ABOUT THIS BOOK

Welcome to the secluded mountain town of Havenwood Falls, home to sexy men, strong women, and neighbors who bite. Discover supernatural mystery, thrills, and romance in a place where everyone has a deep, dark, and often deadly secret.

The second annual Havenwood Falls Short Story Anthology brings a dozen all-new holiday romances to warm you up on these cold winter nights. Curl up by the fire and enjoy paranormal romance tales about shifters, witches, vampires, angels, and other supernatural creatures. Find out who's getting engaged, be a part of the romantic weddings, and even discover a surprise baby!

Celebrate Valentine's Day, Halloween, Thanksgiving, Yule, Christmas, and New Year's with beloved characters, their boyfriends, families, and best friends in your favorite small mountain town. These twelve short stories are all about love, friends, and family, brought to you by nine *USA Today* and Amazon bestselling and award-winning authors in the Havenwood Falls Collective.

Authors include:

- Kristie Cook
- Belinda Boring
- Susan Burdorf
- T.V. Hahn
- E.J. Fechenda
- Morgan Wylie
- Nadirah Foxx
- Seven Jane
- Rose Garcia

DON'T MISS OUT!

Stay up to date at www.HavenwoodFalls.com

Subscribe to our reader group and receive free stories and more!

HAVENWOOD FALLS SHORT STORY ANTHOLOGY 2019

HAVENWOOD FALLS COLLECTIVE

VALENTINE'S DAY 2019

REKINDLED

BY MORGAN WYLIE

A Blackstone Witch Hunters Short Story

$\mathcal{M}$acy Blackstone sat in Coffee Haven, in her favorite front corner booth, and caught up with friends from school—Paisley Underwood, Makenna Walsh, Zara Shannon, Mia Hayes, and of course, Ruby Jean Milton. Since graduating from Havenwood Falls High last summer, Macy had attempted to integrate into the fabric of society as a budding new adult—as her friends had—in their little box canyon town. Her previous job as a barista at Broastful Brew had been perfect for high school, but now Macy intended to learn her family businesses. Destiny had chosen her—and she had finally accepted—to become the next matriarch of the Blackstone family of witch hunters, including oversight of all the businesses. Sure she had her dad and older brother, Brock, to run Stone Falls Winery and Soothing Sips. But it would one day be her responsibility to know the ins and outs of all the Blackstone family enterprises including NamaStays Inn, as well as future seat holder responsibilities with the Court of the Sun and the Moon.

"Hey, Macy, isn't that Gallad diagonal across the street? Over there, near the gazebo and Hey-Nice Glass—and with Rowan Bishop?" Makenna asked with sudden excitement, peering out the window of the coffee shop.

Macy leaned over Paisley, who sat between her, Makenna, and the window for a clear view.

Her eyes widened with surprise. "Sure is. What's he up to, I wonder?"

Macy didn't trust Rowan and couldn't fathom what on earth Gallad could be talking with him about, but she knew they were friends and had been in The Order of the Castors—a secret society Macy was sure was up to no good—with Makenna as well. As far as she knew, they weren't close friends, Although she had been gone for a month their senior year when she left and inadvertently got kidnapped by Dante Blackstone, leader of the rogue witch hunters intent on seeking out and destroying Havenwood Falls—or at least the witches residing within it. She felt a pang in her heart knowing she missed quite a bit in that month and even after as she tried to re-immerse herself into the town and accept her position and fate as a fellow witch hunter—the good kind.

"You could wave him over to say *hi* if you'd like," Mia Hayes offered, with her long dark hair and piercing blue eyes. She had seen her own tragedy in the past year.

"Nah, that's ok. I'll catch up with him later today. Though I do wonder why he's talking with Rowan. I thought he was in New York with Jules."

"It's Rowan Bishop. Who knows. It's probably nothing." Ruby Jean, and Macy's best friend since kindergarten, supplied.

"Maybe. Okay, back to topic." Macy turned around in her seat and faced the girls with a smile. "It's unfortunate Jules and Zaltana couldn't make it back in time to hang with us."

"I think they will make it back in time for the Winterfest, though," Paisley added.

"Good. So, Zara, what's new with you? Any word from Viv and Breckin since they left town?"

4

Zara crossed her arms and rolled her eyes. "Not recently. While they're out livin' it up, I'm stuck here taking online courses and working at Napoli's."

The girls giggled, and all else regarding Gallad was forgotten. But Macy couldn't quite shake the feeling Gallad wasn't telling her about something big. She tried to ignore her instincts while she sipped her latte and chatted with friends, but a sinking feeling was growing in the pit of her stomach.

Ruby Jean grabbed her elbow as they exited Coffee Haven and twisted her away from the other girls into her own confidence.

"What do you think Gallad was doing? Maybe it was a Court errand. Is everything between you two good?" Ruby attempted to whisper.

"Yes, everything's fine, Ruby. At least, I think it is. I don't know what he was doing, but I'm going to find out."

"How? Straight out ask him? That's not very stealthy." Ruby pouted her lip in feigning protest.

Macy laughed. "You want me to be stealthy?"

Her friend nodded with renewed enthusiasm.

Macy paused for a moment in thought. "Perhaps I'll try to follow him today and see if that gets me anywhere. Call me later?"

Ruby nodded with a large Cheshire smile, happy to be in on the conspiracy.

"You are too easily excited by what is most likely nothing."

"It's intrigue. It's excitement. It's . . . it's . . . okay, my life is *so* boring right now. I thought I'd live vicariously through the potential of your scandal."

"You're crazy, you know that?" she called to Ruby, walking backward away from her friend before hitting the square behind her. She moved around the edge of the square. Macy kept her eyes peeled and tuned into her "special" senses. As a born witch hunter, one of her talents allowed her to recognize witches in the vicinity. Now, to Dante Blackstone—brother to her ancestor Marie Blackstone, who helped found Havenwood Falls back in the late 1800s—they used their ability to track, hunt down, and destroy all witches light or dark. Marie had wanted a different kind of life: one she chose, and a community where she could befriend a witch without succumbing to her hunter tendencies. And she did. Marie's descendants had resided in Havenwood Falls ever since.

Over the past year, Macy had been honing her skills to tune out the extra vibrations witches subconsciously gave off in order for her to feel in control while spending time with Gallad. But now, she could easily switch it "on" and pay attention to the vibrations, specifically tuned to the witches of Havenwood Falls. Without skipping a beat, Macy waved and smiled to Cecilia Amundson in the window of Havenwood Falls Music & More while her senses searched the surrounding area. She wasn't sure exactly how far her senses reached, but she could at least scan the entire square.

At first, it was a bit of a shock to her senses to take in all the energies from the nearby witches. Tingles went up her arms into her neck. Immediately she knew she could eliminate the Howe women of Howe's Herbal Shoppe across the square. Randomly, she tuned into a few stragglers who were witches but recognized none of them as Gallad. With no boyfriend in sight, and slightly frustrated she was even attempting to locate him in such a manner, she turned north. She would have called Gallad if she hadn't left her phone at home. Macy pondered stopping at his home, but Gallad still lived with his parents while he worked and studied; he didn't think it made sense to spend his money on a place he spent no time in. This past fall, she had decided to move out of her family home in "The Heights," aka Havenwood Falls Heights, and live on site at the vineyard. From there, she could learn to oversee the business, help Aunt Letti with the Yoga in the Vines classes, and help Aunt Eva run the B&B too. Plus she got a little much-needed space from her mother since they'd been spending so much time together while Macy learned the ropes. It was a win-win for all parties.

With only a few more blocks to go until she reached Blackstone Road, Macy would walk home to the vineyard and get her car before she went to her parents' for dinner. It was Taco Tuesday, and both her brothers Brock and Brice would be there. Gallad came over for other family dinners, but this was the one night just for family.

"Macy would you help set the table?" Lilith Blackstone, Macy's mother, asked. And when Lilith asked, there wasn't much room for anything but the request at hand. She expected people to respond, and they usually did. Lilith wasn't mean or demanding, but her presence was commanding and authoritative. She had to be, holding a seat with the Court of the Sun and the Moon, but also as the matriarch of the family of witch hunters—which in Macy's opinion didn't take much since it was mostly her immediate family and a few distant relatives.

"Brice, grab the taco fixings. We'll start as soon as Brock gets here," Lilith added.

"Which should be any minute," Macy's father, Reggie, chimed in. "I just spoke with him, and he was leaving Soothing Sips." The wine tasting storefront they held downtown on the square—with a secret underground weapons armory—was only minutes away since Brock drove.

Macy looked at each member of her family. Her mom, with whom she shared white-blond hair and bright blue eyes—customary hunter traits—her dad and Brock, the "humans" in the family, who had similar looks with their brown hair and green eyes, and Brice, the only male they had known until last year with dark hair, blue eyes, and the hunter mark. Everyone in their family who had the hunter mark had been female.

Until last year, when Macy met Dante Blackstone. He had several men in his group who had the hunter mark, and none of them had light hair. Although, the blue eyes seemed to be a consistent trait. Macy's parents had been looking into why Brice was the only male in their line to have the hunter's mark appear. She didn't think it was a coincidence Brice's middle name happened to be Dante. In her opinion, her mom knew more than she let on. But that was another story. Macy sighed. Her family definitely had their flaws, but she loved them.

"Hey, Brock? Did you see Gallad in town today? I thought I saw him but didn't get to him in time. He seemed to be acting strange, kind of secretive." Macy asked around a bite of taco.

Brice jumped in with a snarky retort. "Geez, Macy, don't you trust him?"

Macy leaned back almost offended. "Of course I do. It just seemed strange, that's all."

"No, sorry, Mace, the Sip was pretty slammed today. I barely took my breaks," Brock said.

"Macy, dear, perhaps you should simply ask him yourself?" her mother wisely asked. But something about the way her eyes slid toward her dad bothered Macy.

"I will. I was just curious."

"Well, perhaps he was on Court business," her mother added, with a suspicious undertone.

"Do you know something, Mother?"

"It's not my business."

"If it's Court business, I'm pretty sure it's your business too."

Lilith stared Macy down for a fraction of a second before turning toward her untouched taco.

Macy sighed and rambled out, "I'm afraid the Court is going to make him go on a mission, errand, or whatever outside of Havenwood Falls. It's dangerous out there, as we all know. Dante and the others are still out there somewhere, looking for any chance to find us."

A collective, yet subconscious, sigh was released around the table.

"Macy, Gallad is a strong and smart witch. The Court wouldn't put him unnecessarily at risk. They know what's out there," Macy's dad encouraged.

"I'll find out what I can," her mom offered. "But in the meantime, I suggest you wait to hear from Gallad. It's quite an honor, you know, to be chosen. It means they have faith in his abilities and his future prospects."

"You're right. And if he's going to become the leader of his family's coven and hold their seat, I would have to get used to all the dangers and things involved with that." Macy inhaled deeply to calm down. Nodding to herself, decision made, she then continued to eat her taco.

"These are great, Mom. Thanks for the tacos," Brock added, practically swallowing the entire taco in a single bite, causing the rest to laugh, lightening the mood and all the supernatural chat around the table. She loved her brother. It pained her to see Brock without the family's abilities, but she knew he had come to terms in his own way.

"Brice, are you on your phone?" Reggie asked, with a frown at his youngest son.

Brice scrambled to put his phone in his pocket and nervously flashed his eyes toward his mom, who nodded imperceptibly. Macy barely caught the action. *Hmm, something is up with those two.*

"Sorry, Dad."

"Put it away, son. Rule is no phones at the table. No matter what." Reggie gave Brice a strange look.

Brice put his hands on the table as if to show no phone within them. He smiled big at Brock, who threw a piece of lettuce at Brice's face, causing a fit of giggles from around the table. The rest of the evening passed uneventfully with Macy hoping to call Gallad as soon as she left.

"Macy! Hey, Macy!" a voice called. Ruby Jean had just passed Whisper Falls Inn, heading into the square the next day.

Macy had an errand to run for her Aunt Letti in town—something about supplies for NamaStays Inn, but Aunt Letti had a mischievous glint in her eyes. According to her list, she needed to place an order with Howe's Herbal Shoppe. She also had to drop off a case of the "special" bottles of wine at Soothing Sips for Brock. While the winery boasted wonderful choices for all kinds—humans included—they also secretly made special variations for the vampires, fae, and other races of beings who resided in Havenwood Falls.

"Hey, girl, what are you up to today? Any more conspiracy theories with your knight in shining armor?" Ruby Jean winked and linked her arm within Macy's, elbow to elbow.

Macy laughed. "No. And hello to you! What are you up to today?"

"Oh, a little of this and a little of that."

Macy gave her a questioning look.

"Okay, so I'm bored out of my mind and had to get out of the house." She rolled her eyes and laughed. "But I'm getting good exercise wandering the square!"

"That's good. Ruby Jean, why don't you get a job? You had some interviews lined up. What happened?"

Ruby Jean paused, her face fallen. "I just wasn't right for them."

Macy stopped abruptly and swung her friend about face. "You didn't even interview! How would you know?"

Unable to look Macy in the eyes, she shrugged her shoulders. "I just know. I'm not like you, Macy. I don't know what I want to be or where I fit yet."

Swiftly, apparently not wanting to talk about it further, Ruby Jean's face lit up. "Let's go to Burger Bar and get milkshakes. Do you have time?"

Macy frowned, concerned for her best friend. She glanced at her phone to see the time. "Let me place my order with Mrs. Howe, then we can go after I drop off a shipment for Brock. But, Ruby Jean, we are not finished with this discussion yet."

Ruby nodded, but smiled at the prospect of a milkshake. "I'll help you with your errands, 'kay?"

Macy and Ruby Jean headed across the square to Howe's Herbal Shoppe.

"How can I— Oh hello, Macy, Ruby Jean. What can I do for you today?" Mrs. Ruby Howe asked. She stood hunched over a hidden book behind the counter as she stirred something.

"That smells so good." Ruby Jean inhaled.

"Thank you, dear. Best not to smell too deeply, as you're still quite young." She finished with a wink, but her words caused Macy to step up beside her friend to change the subject. One was never quite sure what the elder Mrs. Howe was up to. She had times of lucidity, but more often than not lately, her words could be jumbled conversations mixed with spells. Macy didn't plan on spending too much time in the shop. Just in case.

"Oh, hey, Macy and Ruby Jean!" Scarlet came in from the back room and patted her grandmother on the shoulder. "I'll help Macy out, Gram. She's a friend from school, remember?"

"Of course I remember. I'm not the senile old fool you all think I am." She giggled but didn't take her eyes off whatever was in the pot she was stirring so diligently.

"I never said you were!" Scarlet replied with disgust but winked at Macy. She stepped out from behind the counter, her long red hair braided down either side of her neck. Her pale complexion highlighted a spattering of freckles across her nose.

"Hey, Scarlet, thanks. I just have an order from Aunt Letti for the vineyard and the inn. We are in need of some candles, soaps, and lotions, it looks like," Macy said as she scanned the list she was given, then handed it to Scarlet.

Scarlet, the youngest of the Howe witches, went to school with the girls, but was a year behind them. She was very sweet and could often be found with her friend/boyfriend—Macy was never sure if they were public or not—Bale, a dragon shifter. They made a great couple. She didn't know why they played it down so much, though she gathered it had something to do with Bale's family.

"No problem. We can take care of this. Some of these requests we don't have in stock so it will take a couple hours to get them ready. Is that okay?" Scarlet asked.

"Sure, that's what I figured. Ruby Jean and I were going to go to Burger Bar and get a shake. Would you like us to bring you one back?"

"No thanks, I'm good!" Scarlet turned with a flourish and headed to gather the supplies she would need to complete the order. "See you in a couple hours!"

Macy and Ruby Jean waved and headed out the door into the cold frigid air with the sound of a bell dinging behind them as the door clanged shut. Ruby held her hands palm outstretched.

"It's starting to snow again," she said with childlike wonder.

"You are the strangest cat shifter I've ever met," Macy said with a laugh. "Most don't like the snow or the cold."

Ruby Jean shrugged her shoulders. "What can I say? I'm an original!"

"Come on. One more stop! I parked the truck in front of Sips."

They each carried a box full of wine bottles into Soothing Sips wine tasting shop and were greeted by more than one smiling male at the counter as they walked in.

"Hey, Macy! Let me help you with that. Hi, Ruby Jean!" Gallad said, quickly moving to take the boxes, one in each hand, and place them on the counter.

"Hey, yourself! What are you doing here? I was about to give up on you not answering my calls," she scolded him.

He had the decency to look ashamed and dropped his head. But when he tipped his head to look up at her, she was affronted with puppy-dog eyes and a smirk that could—and did—get him anything he wanted.

"I'm sorry, Mace." He lovingly gripped both her shoulders. "But that's why I'm here. I wanted to surprise you. I ran into your dad at the winery. He said you were on your way here. So here I am." Proudly he expected full forgiveness, which, of course, he got.

Macy stood up on her tip toes, wrapped her arms around his neck, and kissed his cheek.

"Forgiven. Now you boys get the other boxes so us fragile, weak women can stand here, look pretty, and fan ourselves."

"Nice, Mace." Her brother, Brock, laughed as he opened the tailgate of the small work truck.

When they were finished, Brock got to work stacking the bottles he needed to replenish stock, then he took the more private stock—most of which were special orders that wouldn't appeal to the humans of Havenwood Falls—into the back room.

"So what are you two up to today?" Gallad asked, including Ruby Jean in the conversation.

Ruby smiled. "Well, we thought we might head to Burger Bar after this and get a shake. Would you like to join us?"

Macy watched his reaction, but there wasn't much to take note of. The guy was smooth as silk and didn't miss a beat.

"Thank you, but I have some work to do for the Court today. Raincheck?"

"What do they have you working on? Or is it top secret?" Macy asked, annoyed she didn't get the time she used to with him before being the Court's errand boy. But in his words, he was putting in his time and gaining their respect for when it was his time to join their ranks.

"It *is* top secret," Gallad whispered conspiratorially. "I could tell you, but then you know what I'd have to do you, right?"

"Kill her?" Ruby Jean excitedly asked, then realized what she had said at Macy's frown. But she waved her off to have her fun.

"No, I'd have to"—Gallad grabbed Macy's hand and spun her into his chest—"I'd have to dance with her."

Ruby groaned in disappointment. But Gallad spun Macy back out, pushed her under his arm in a twist, then dropped her in a deep dip, knowing how much she didn't like dancing. But Macy laughed, which was what he was apparently after. He kissed her forehead, then brought her upright. She smacked his arm playfully then quickly sobered and pouted.

"Gallad, when can I see you? I miss you."

"Me too." He laced his fingers through hers. "Which is what brought me here today. I came to ask you to dinner tomorrow night. I have some things I need to talk to you about regarding the Court and something they have planned for me. Are you free tomorrow?"

"For you? Anytime. Just tell me when to be ready." She smiled.

"Great. Tomorrow seven p.m. I'll come get you at the vineyard."

"Are we talking Napoli's attire or something else?" Macy asked. A girl has to know how to dress.

Gallad thought for a moment. "How does Fallview Tavern sound?"

Macy smiled and nodded. Gallad said his goodbyes then left the store.

"Come on, Mace! We have to find a dress for you to wear!" Ruby

Jean practically dragged her from the store with barely time for a wave to Brock.

"What about shakes?"

"Forget shakes—we need to shop! We can grab coffee then head to Callie's Consignment. I love her clothes!" Ruby was excited, and she wasn't even going.

Macy couldn't help the feeling of dread that came over her. Something was going on, and tomorrow was the moment she would find out what it was—her gut was telling her she wouldn't like it.

"Hey, Callie!" Ruby called over the ding when they walked in the door.

Macy inhaled deeply. She loved the smell inside Callie's store—a mix of the old, new, and something stronger . . . an underlying scent that was uniquely Callie. Macy thought it had something to do with her gypsy heritage.

"What brings you two into my store on this flippin' cold January day?" Callie asked, putting aside some new stock she looked to be separating on the counter.

"We are on the hunt for a new date dress for Macy!" Ruby Jean beamed. Macy wanted to roll her eyes at her best friend but couldn't bring herself to take the joy away from her. "Do you have anything new we should see? Or just point us in the right direction, and we'll figure it out."

"I just got in a new shipment yesterday that held some beautiful, um, 'date dresses,' as you called them." Callie pinched her face. "Although, knowing Macy's style is a little more retro casual, you might also try that middle section. There are some amazing new jackets, too!" The bangles on Callie's arms clinked as she pointed her hand to the back of the room.

Macy had to admit the idea of a new jacket made her happy they had stopped in. She would rather wear her jeans and a T-shirt, but for Gallad, she would dress up to the best she could stomach.

"Thanks, Callie," both girls responded, following her directions.

"Let me know if you need help!"

An hour later, both Macy and Ruby Jean had found a few articles they couldn't leave without. But as they paid, Callie zoned in on Macy's face for the briefest moment. Her eyes shifted, and she bit her lip.

"What? What is it, Callie?" Macy asked, suddenly concerned. She knew some of Callie's abilities included reading people.

"Don't wear this tomorrow. Save it for the Winter Carnival. And don't ask what I saw. You know I don't share the visions." She finished ringing them up as if what she said wasn't a big deal. Macy nodded, a bit shaken Callie felt anything for her at all.

"Have fun, ladies!" Callie called as they reached the door.

"Bye, Callie, thanks!"

"So that was weird," Ruby added, walking to the truck.

"Yep."

"Now you need to wear something else you already have tomorrow."

"Yep."

"You going to be okay?" Ruby asked, concern coloring her face. Macy opened her mouth, but Ruby stopped her. "If you say 'yep' one more time, I'm going to strangle you."

Macy laughed.

"That's better. I can come home with you and help you look, if you want?"

"That's okay, Ruby. I'll be fine. I think I need some time alone anyway. I have a weird feeling about dinner tomorrow." Macy pinched the bridge of her nose and closed her eyes.

Ruby Jean inhaled sharply. "Oh . . . oh . . . do you think he's going to propose to you?"

"No. I actually think it's bad news. Or news that would take Gallad away from Havenwood Falls for a time, and that makes me nervous."

"Well, you better call me the minute you get home from your date tomorrow night. Promise?" Ruby stuck out her pinky.

Macy latched her pinky within her friends. "Promise."

"You look gorgeous, Macy," Gallad said barely above a whisper. He moved in close to her, practically prowling. She giggled as he cupped his hand around her dainty neck. Her long flowing locks pinned up loosely, appearing white with the snow as her background. She found the perfect combination outfit of a sparkling pink sleeveless top complete with a short long-sleeved white sweater, leading down to her black leather pants and black wedge booties.

"Thank you. You don't look too shabby yourself," Macy said with a smile.

They matched quite nicely with his unbuckled black boots meeting the base of his dark gray stone-washed jeans, black T-shirt, and black leather jacket, with a manly moonstone and leather-roped necklace, peeking out from the collar. Gallad never disappointed in the looks department. She had always appreciated the dichotomy that was Gallad: sexy smart in a bad boy package. His thick dark hair on top had a mind of its own, and his deep green eyes drew the attention to all his masculine features. But his smile was charm and wickedness all in one.

He carefully grabbed her hand in one of his and her elbow with the other as he assisted her into the car. They drove in companionable silence until they reached the Fallview Tavern, and he took her inside.

"Macy, I wanted to talk to you about something that's been brewing—see what I did there?" he chuckled lamely, knowing it was a bad attempt at a joke.

"Ha. Ha. Very funny. Now get on with it. My stomach's been in agony waiting to see what you've been keeping from me," Macy admitted.

"So you noticed that, did you?" Gallad bit the inside of his cheek. "I'm sorry, Macy. I just wasn't able to disclose it yet. But I thought it was time to bring you in the loop now." Macy nodded, nervously staring deep into Gallad's eyes, watching everything she could about him. Gallad lowered his voice and leaned in close to keep his voice down. "The Luna Coven and the Court of the Sun and the Moon have asked if I would be willing to accompany some on a mission of sorts— really it's an undercover information gathering trip outside Havenwood Falls. There have been whispers of information regarding the Collector's network of supporters. They are sending inconspicuous people who can do research and will know what to look for."

Macy's mouth fell open. It was almost worse than she originally thought. Dante Blackstone was one thing, but the Collector was an entirely different other. No one knew how far the Collector's influence reached. Not to mention the shapeshifter and Rachelle, the hellhound-witch associated with the Collector, were still MIA. Macie only knew this because of her own training with her mother.

"Don't worry. It won't be dangerous."

"How can you say that? After everything that recently went down with the Collector . . . you have no idea what it will be." Macy's voice held a hint of panic.

Gallad reached across and held her hand. She felt his magic flow into her, attempting to instill some calm. Macy closed her eyes and inhaled slow deep breaths. Her eyes opened, and she nodded with new determination.

"Okay. You know I support you and I believe in you fully. I just wish you didn't have to leave."

"It won't be for too long."

"When do you go?"

"Monday, the day after Winterfest. So at least I'll get to go to that with you." Gallad smiled. His smile could melt the iciest heart. Macy couldn't help but smile in return, even though her heart hurt with the prospect of him leaving on such a dangerous mission—whether he wanted to admit it or not.

"Oh, Macy, you look fab! That's the outfit we got at Callie's, the one she told you to wear tonight!" Ruby Jean said with an excited clap.

Macy had met her and their other friends at their appointed meeting place by the gazebo, which was decorated with large glowing snowflakes and the banner announcing Winterfest 2019. They planned to meet as a group to peruse the ice and snow sculpture entries, then after gather to hang out at the vineyard.

"Thank you!" Macy laughed and twirled whimsically to show off the light pink sheer layers upon layers that made up her ankle-length skirt. This time she accompanied it with a fuzzy black short sweater over a pink cami. It was, of course, freezing so she had on a long black wool coat, and her hair was left down, cascading white ringlets around her shoulders.

Gallad approached, his eyes only for Macy; in them she saw his want and desire. For her.

Heat flooded her body from her head down to her toes, and suddenly her wool coat was too much. He stalked toward her. His long legs, lithe and sure with every step. He was a vision in black—black sweater, black jacket, black jeans, and black boots. Only his green eyes stood out against the pale backdrop of his skin and was complimented by his dark hair, collecting tiny flakes of white shimmering in the air, as if by magic.

He was in her space, breathing her in before a word was uttered.

"Hi," he whispered.

"Hi," she returned, a blush creeping up her neck, uncomfortable with the PDA right in front of their friends. Unable to take her eyes from his, she heard the others around them clear their throats, reminding them of their presence. They moved apart, Gallad still clinging to her hand.

"Well, are we all here? Should we go check out the ice sculptures?" Ruby Jean asked with pure excitement.

Macy noted Scarlet and Bale standing close enough that their arms touched, Willa Kasun and Tarron Wilde, Paisley, Makenna, and a few others standing about. "I think we can just check things out together or separate and then meet back up at the end, right?"

"Right," Gallad interjected. "I think there are too many of us to actually walk through the aisles together."

"That sounds cool, man," Bale agreed with a fist bump to Gallad as he gently steered Scarlet over to a sculpture of a dragon she was eyeing.

The rest either went their separate ways or tagged along until they found something more interesting. Ruby Jean and Willa chatted about a particular display of ice that appeared to look like a castle used as a famous fiction witchcraft school. Others looked on with wonder at some unknown mice scene which won first place, and a giant winged lion which won second for Harper Sinclair and Elias Jamison.

"Gallad, isn't this amazing?" Macy looked around in awe at all the sculptures. The night was perfect, if a bit cold. The snow had started to come down in bigger flakes, and the twinkle lights the town had set up for the carnival made it all look so magical.

"It is," he agreed. Macy looked up at him. Something about him seemed preoccupied tonight. She watched him give a "what's up" to Rowan Bishop passing down another aisle.

"Are you nervous about your mission? Or is something else bothering you?" she curiously asked.

He smiled down at her—being a whole head taller than she—and kissed her forehead. "You could say I'm a bit nervous. But not about what you think." He stopped her in the middle of an aisle of people and grabbed her hand, lacing his between her delicate fingers. "Macy, come walk with me? I'd like to spend time with you alone for a bit."

"I thought you'd never ask!" She winked at him and let him lead her through the throngs of people, away from the carnival and to his awaiting car.

"It's too cold to walk there dressed how we are. We'll drive for a bit then walk."

"Okay. Where to?"

"The falls."

Gallad took Macy's hand and led her to the trailhead beyond the mansions of Havenwood Heights where both their founding families had settled.

"It's much darker out here away from the town lights," Macy mentioned as they began their ascent toward the falls.

"Much quieter too," Gallad added with a smile. They both laughed at the crunching sound of the snow beneath their feet.

Macy released Gallad's hand, ran playfully ahead of him, and spun in a circle with her arms outstretched. "It's so magical, Gallad."

Large snowflakes had started falling again. Gallad grabbed her and pulled her to his chest, then kissed her fully on the mouth until they both breathed heavily.

They continued walking toward the pool at the base of the great falls. Ice crystals formed on the tree branches and low lying shrubbery all around them, a tinkling sound added to the natural and supernatural magical sounds of the forest. The snow continued to accumulate on the ground, the flakes illuminating their surroundings. The pathway magically cleared before them, and as they neared the site, the soft hush of the whispering falls tickled their ears.

"Oh Gallad, I haven't been up here yet this winter. The falls are amazing." Macy looked around and absorbed all she could take in. The falls were but a trickle compared to the rush of the water in the spring. Edges of solid packed ice guided the remaining water to the pool below.

"They are," he agreed. Following her line of sight until his gaze landed on the pool. A moment passed, and Macy gasped and rushed toward the edge of the pool. Emerging out of the dark, hundreds of illuminated candles floating in the water and rising into the sky lit the area with a magical glow. The ice crystals in the trees and in the air reflected the light sparkling on the snow surrounding them.

Macy paused, then turned to Gallad with a reverent expression of awe. "Are you doing this?"

Gallad smiled, the same smile that turned Macy's brain to mush and sent the butterflies in her stomach into a flurry.

Suddenly, Gallad was before her on one knee, taking Macy's hand in his own. He bent his head down and kissed the back of her hand—a slow, meaningful kiss full of intention and desire.

"Macy Blackstone, I love you with all my heart and soul. I would follow you to the ends of the earth and always ensure you can find your way home. Will you do me the honor of being my wife?"

Macy gazed into his eyes. Green eyes full of sincerity, love, and loyalty. She couldn't help but remember when he was the only key to bringing her home when Dante had held her, using her as bait to find Havenwood Falls.

Gallad was her heart. Her home.

"Yes. You are the other half to my soul. I am always home with you."

He placed a ring on her finger, and she leapt onto him, wrapping her arms around his neck as he stood to his feet. He held her and twirled her around, his face buried in her neck. Macy couldn't help the exuberant burst of joy that bubbled from her chest.

She pulled back when he placed her back on the ground. "Wait. Aren't you leaving town tomorrow? I want time with you."

Gallad's face became boyishly sheepish. "Well, that may have been a bit of a lie. See, I was trying to keep this all a secret. I needed a couple spells, and I needed you not to find out. But Brice let me know what you thought was going on, so I ran with it to throw you off. Are you mad?"

"So you're not leaving town?"

"Not anytime soon." Gallad shrugged his shoulders as if unconcerned.

"Then no, I'm thrilled!" She leaned up on her toes and playfully kissed his chin. She smiled then wrapped her arms around his as they enjoyed the magical scenery.

She leaned her head against his shoulder. "This is the same spot my ancestors Marie and Judson Blackstone were officially engaged so many years ago when they first came to Havenwood Falls in the 1850s. I'm sure they didn't have all this." Macy gestured out with her hands toward the lights. "But it does make it that much more special."

Once they arrived at the vineyard to meet their friends after the winter carnival, Macy realized there were many more people there than originally planned. The winery and tasting room were fully decorated. Multiple barrels with small fires were scattered about, and plates of food and bottles of wine adorned the tables. As they entered the area, Macy was rushed by her friends, Ruby Jean chief among them.

"Macy Marie Blackstone! Did you just get yourself engaged?" she asked.

Macy held out her hand to show her the ring, and Ruby screamed and jumped up and down.

"Did you not know about all this?" Macy asked, gesturing to the awaiting party.

With hands on her hips, Ruby glared at Gallad. "No."

Gallad huffed unapologetically with a smile. "Sorry. You know you would have told her, Ruby."

She blushed but conceded his point.

Macy and Gallad were surrounded with friends and family who had come to celebrate them. She spotted her parents talking with Gallad's. Her brother Brock helped serve the tables, bringing out more food while Brice and his friends played with a hacky sack off to the side. Gianna, Gallad's sister, was among them. Their cousins Harlow and Taylor, their parents, and his grandparents Mathilde and Del visited in front of a fire. Michaela Petran, Addie Beaumont—who was also his cousin—and Callie helped themselves and enjoyed the wine. So many she had grown up with and grown to love and appreciate were here to support her and her future with Gallad. Macy's family with those of Gallad's were now a rekindled version of what their ancestors had set out to accomplish: a place where, among others, witches and witch hunters could live peacefully and coexist together as a community.

This was her home. Her family. And she couldn't wait to start her future with Gallad in Havenwood Falls.

Have you read all of the Blackstone Witch Hunters stories?

Reawakened by Morgan Wylie
Dawn of the Witch Hunters by Morgan Wylie
Redefined by Morgan Wylie
Rise of the Witch Hunters by Morgan Wylie
Rediscovered by Morgan Wylie

TRUSTING THE BEAST

BY SF BENSON WRITING AS NADIRAH FOXX

A Hunter & Izzy Short Story

J'd never been a big fan of diamonds, and the extravagance associated with them. The rock on my left hand, however, wasn't a symbol of lavishness. Hunter said he picked out the two-carat pear-shaped solitaire because he wanted everyone to know we were engaged. I would have preferred to skip the ring—announcements weren't necessary.

Not that I didn't want to marry Hunter James. With each day that passed, I loved him more and more. I just wasn't a fan of public displays of any sort. Besides, we were still getting to know each other. The proposal was too soon.

Hunter and I decorated the tree on Christmas Eve. We'd been so busy with events around town that we'd forgotten about our own celebration. As I hung a satiny silver bulb, I saw a tiny white box, and my heart skipped a beat.

"Open it," he said, coming over to me.

My hands shook as I removed the red ribbon. Inside the box was a perfect yet enormous engagement ring.

He reached over, took it from me, and went down on one knee. "Izzie Itzae, meeting you was the best thing to ever happen to me. You were a vision come true. I don't wish to spend another moment without you in my life. Be my wife. Marry me."

"Yes!" The word rushed from my lips.

It wasn't until after the ring was in place, and we were sharing a champagne toast with Hunter's grandfather that I thought about what I'd done. I remembered how my father deserted us. And I never forgot Mom's warning—nagual males aren't trustworthy. Instead of admitting my doubts, I went along with the situation and hoped for the best.

Senora, my best friend, was helping me plan the spring wedding. She was closer to me than any of my family. My siblings and grandparents had their own lives and weren't concerned about me. When I was seventeen, Dad abandoned us and then Mom died. Because of the turmoil in my life, Senora wanted me to have the wedding of every girl's dreams. Sadly, I considered finding a mate, tying the knot, and having a family the stuff of nightmares. All I envisioned was following in my parents' footsteps. Mom loved a coward. Her love for him broke her heart and hastened her death. The state troopers found her car crashed on the side of a hill.

The totem around my neck warmed as Hunter entered the great room. I turned away from the patio door as he came closer.

"Hey, *cariño*." Hunter wrapped his arms around my waist, pulling me in close, and kissing me.

Despite my apprehension, I wouldn't trade his affection for anything.

He broke off the kiss and said against my lips, "Baba's had another vision."

"Oh?" The shaman hadn't had a vision since that nasty ordeal with Cheresse Winters.

"He saw a woman on the road leading into Havenwood Falls. She's by herself and appears to be hurt."

It piqued my interest, but I didn't understand why Hunter felt the need to tell me. "Isn't this something SIN or someone from the Court should check out?"

"Yeah, but Baba said he felt a connection between you and the woman."

His words tied a knot in my gut. I wasn't close to anyone else in Colorado other than Senora, Hunter, and his grandfather, and they were in the house. "Where is she?"

"Still out there." Hunter glanced out the glass door. "It'll be dark soon. We should go find her while we can. Baba and I pinpointed the area."

Night fell before we found the stranger. Relying on our heightened senses, we split up and searched the forest along the two-lane county road. Last time I was here, my rented vehicle suddenly died, and my savior came in the form of a redheaded wench.

A soft moan snagged my attention. When I saw nothing, I turned toward Hunter's pickup, but then I heard it again coming from a ravine. I sent a mental message to Hunter as I ran toward the noise. Navigating the woods as a puma was a lot easier than in human form. It amazed me how graceful I was as an animal, but on two legs I was as clumsy as a toddler learning to walk.

"Help me." The faint voice was feminine.

In a matter of seconds, Hunter appeared at my side. "Did you hear that?"

"Yeah. It's coming from the right."

He reached for my hand and tugged me along—his sight much better than mine. It didn't take long for us to reach the woman. Clad in a jacket and jeans, her body was twisted in an unnatural angle.

"Hey, we're here to help," Hunter said, crouching beside her. He pushed a large branch off her leg. "You may have some broken bones. Try not to move."

The woman dragged a hand up to her neck. That's when I noticed the totem. She was another nagual. As I moved closer, butterflies took off in my stomach and my heart raced. Familiarity wafted off the female, but that couldn't be possible. I spoke to my sister a week ago, and she was on her way to Europe—another reason why I wasn't troubling her about my wedding. I didn't know any other naguals.

Not alive.

The woman ignored Hunter's advice and struggled to sit up. "Thank you. I couldn't get it off."

I gasped. That voice. It couldn't be. Grandmother said she died, but we never found a body.

The woman glanced up at me and confirmed my worst fears. "Izzie? Is that you?"

"Mom?"

The ride back into town was a silent one with Mom resting in the back seat. Every few miles, Hunter glanced over at me. I couldn't speak. If I did, all the anger built up in me would tumble out, and I'd say words that I could never take back. She was alive and never contacted me.

"Izzie?" he said.

"Not now. Not here."

As soon as Hunter pulled into the garage, I jumped out and ran inside, nearly knocking over Baba.

"Did you locate her?" he said to my back.

I didn't stop moving until I reached the deck. This had to be the world's worst nightmare. How could my mother be alive?

The door opened behind me, and two sets of footsteps clumped across the wooden floor. A hand touched the small of my back. Hunter spoke in a lowered voice. "I'm confused, Izzie. I thought she was dead."

He wasn't the only one baffled.

I whirled around, letting my eyes travel over my mother. Outside of her matted dark hair and tired hazel eyes, she appeared unharmed. Undoubtedly, her healing abilities kicked in after being freed from the branch. She didn't look a day older than she did nine years ago. I leaned against the railing and folded my arms over my chest. Instead of feeling gratitude, my anger grew.

"So where have you been, Mom? Did you get lost going to the hospital?" The morning she disappeared, Mom claimed to be going to work—she was a nurse. "Or maybe you forgot how to get to the school? Remember the kids you were supposed to pick up that afternoon?"

"Let me explain, Izzie." She lifted a hand to touch me.

"Don't!" I stepped over, out of her reach. "Do you know what shit you put us through? Grandmother died a year after you left. I had to raise myself and my siblings! Why did you do this to us?"

Hunter motioned for me to calm down, but I couldn't.

Mom sighed. "I-I wasn't coping well with your father's disappearance. Every day I spent—"

"Lame, Mom." I pushed off the railing and walked to the far side of the porch. "You thought more of yourself than your children? So damned lame . . . and irresponsible."

Hunter cleared his throat and scratched his head. "Why don't I go get Addie? We can talk later."

He rushed over to the door as if he were glad to be leaving.

"You should get used to that," Mom said with a fist on her hip.

"What the hell are you talking about?" My beast was pushing forth, wanting to express her thoughts about Mom's sudden reappearance.

Her gaze traveled down my arm, and then back up to my face. "If you're going to marry a nagual, remember the males don't know how to stick around."

"I guess you would be the expert at that," I said curtly.

Mom shook her head. "Think what you will, but I left you in good hands. My mother was a much better mother than I could be."

"Grandmother didn't raise us, Mom. If it weren't for me . . ." I'd had enough. I headed for the door.

Mom stopped me with a hand on my arm. "I had no choice. Without my mate, I was dying inside. I had to find your father."

"Did you?" A spark of hope ignited. Even my beast held her breath. "Did you find him, Mom?"

"I came close a few times. I followed him all the way to Spain. About a year ago, he returned to the States—to Colorado." She lowered her trembling hand. "I found him. He told me I was foolish. He had a new family—a wife and kids—and didn't need us."

Her news sickened me. My father didn't care. Just replaced us like we were fucking furniture or some shit. "Why didn't *you* come back?"

"Embarrassed. Without a job, I'd burned through the money I'd stashed."

"So how did you live?"

She shrugged. "You don't want to know. I've done things that I'm not proud of. When you found me, I was on the run from a man who abused me."

When I tried to hug her, Mom stepped back.

"I don't want your sympathy. Just help me get back on my feet, and I'll leave you alone."

"Sure, Mom." This time when I reached for her, she allowed the gesture.

Addie wasted no time coming by the house to do Mom's tattoo. I left them alone in the guest room and went out to the deck with Hunter. He was desperate to talk about what was going on while all I wanted was a quick run to work off pent-up emotions.

"What's the deal with your mom?" Hunter asked as he leaned his forearms on the railing. "Did she explain her absence?"

"She claimed to be searching for my dad. When she found him, she discovered he had lived a life without us. New wife and kids."

"Damn."

"Yeah." I tipped my head back, looked up into the night sky, and inhaled the relaxing scent of burning pine. We were expecting snow again, and the air was crisp. My beast wanted out. Why were we talking instead of running?

Hunter, however, continued the Q and A. "So where has she been all this time?"

"Mom said she was with someone who abused her. When we found her, she was trying to get away."

"You sound like you don't believe her," Hunter said.

I shrugged. "Honestly? Who knows? Mom said she did things she wasn't proud of. I've been there. But I'm not buying the-looking-for-my-father story."

Hunter stood and faced me. "We've all done questionable shit, but family doesn't desert each other."

"Duh!"

He shook his head. "Not what I meant, *cariño*. She needs our help."

I slipped my hands around his waist. "I said I'd help her get back on her feet. Maybe if I pay her enough, she'll disappear permanently."

"Izzie, you don't mean that." He hugged me tightly. "We'll help your mom. Maybe SIN can get involved and find the asshole who hurt her. If we can do it safely, we'll help your mom get settled somewhere outside Havenwood Falls. That is, if you want it."

"Sounds good." Resting my head against Hunter's chest, I wished it could be so simple.

The next morning, Mom proved that nothing with her was easy. She entered the kitchen complaining loud enough to wake the dead.

"Mom!" I rushed into the room. "What's wrong?"

"There's nothing to eat here! I'm starving!" Mom stood in the center of the room with her hands on her hips and her waist-length black hair swinging side to side.

Gripping the edge of the granite counter, I noticed all the food

Baba had prepared. A wonderful buffet—scrambled eggs with chorizo, homemade salsa, fry bread, grilled ham, a fruit bowl, and even a fresh pot of coffee—sat on the island. Did Mom lose her vision or her mind?

"Mom, chill." I wanted to shout, but doing so would be like throwing lighter fluid on a fire. Maybe she wanted something different. "Is there something you want that's not here?"

"How about pancakes, bacon, eggs without that greasy-ass meat?"

I drew in a deep breath and counted to ten. It had been years since we'd been around each other. People changed. I didn't know what Mom liked or disliked anymore. "Give me a few minutes, and I'll make you something else. Perhaps you could have a cup of coffee—"

"I prefer tea."

"What the fuck is going on?" said Senora as she shuffled into the room. Although she rarely got up before noon, my bestie was a light sleeper.

This wasn't the way I wanted to introduce them, but Mom left me little choice. "Senora meet Nita. Mom, this is my best friend."

The two females sized each other up as if they were about to go to war. Senora broke the ice. "I thought you were dead."

Mom narrowed her eyes. "And I thought your kind reigned in Hell."

Shit. Not good. "Senora, can I speak to you outside?"

She cast a golden gaze toward my mother before pushing past me. Senora had promised the Court that she wouldn't eat anyone else without permission, but if Mom didn't curb her attitude, Senora might rescind the vow. I didn't want that on my conscience.

"Mom, you're welcome to make whatever you'd like for breakfast. If you don't see something, call out for Baba to help you." I didn't wait for her response as I hurried out to speak to Senora.

As soon as I opened the door, she lit into me. "When that female disappeared, who helped you?"

"My grandmother."

Senora leaned a hip against the railing. "And when she died?"

"You did."

31

"Damn, Izzie. I've been by your side for years. I helped you keep a fucking roof over your head and put food on your table."

"I know, I know."

"Do you?" Senora folded her arms. "I'm picking up bad vibes from her, and I don't like it. Watch your back around that female."

"I will."

My bestie bobbed her head. "I'm going back to bed."

I watched my friend duck back into the house. Keeping my mother around might not be the best decision I'd ever made.

Attempting to smooth things over with Mom, I took her to Pleasurez. There was a new shipment coming in, plus I had a meeting with Reyna, a new lingerie designer in town. She was working on a lingerie show at Silk, and my shop was handling the sales. Plus, Pleasurez was expanding to an online store, and I wanted to sell her designs there, too.

It was a quiet morning, so I took my time putting away the merchandise with Mom's help.

"So, you own this place?" Mom asked as she perused a Valentine's Day display of sex toys.

"Hunter and I own it together," I said and turned my attention to a box of lacy bralettes.

Mom put her hand on mine, forcing me to glance up. "Have you thought hard about marrying this male?"

The knot that formed the night we rescued Mom grew tighter. "Mom, we love each other. He's my soul mate—"

"That's an overrated philosophy. Your father is proof of that."

My beast clawed beneath the surface. "Let's not go there."

Mom ignored me and continued on with her rant. "Marrying Hunter is a bad idea. Things will be great between you, and then he'll get you knocked up. As soon as the kits are born, that male of yours will hit the road. Nagual shifters aren't loyal."

Why did she have to speak to the very fears I was dealing with? Deep down, my beast wanted to argue. She believed in Hunter. In *us*.

Thankfully, the bell over the door sounded. Reyna entered, and this conversation was over.

For now.

The next two days I listened to Mom's incessant badgering. She didn't have a positive word to say about marriage, my father, and especially Hunter. My own worries grew with her constant jabbering. They became palpable and settled in my gut, making me sick. I spent the third day in bed.

"Can we talk?" Hunter stood in the bedroom doorway.

Making things worse was the fact that Hunter and I had lost our connection. Our intimacy ceased. We didn't even go on one run. Too ashamed to face him, I rolled over on my side.

The mattress dipped. "Talk to me, *cariño*. Have I done something?"

"No."

He sighed. "Then it's Nita. Right?"

I sat up and looked down at my hand. It was now or never. I tugged on the ring and held it out to him. "I can't do this. I was wrong thinking I could be normal and marry you."

A lesser male would argue his case or simply agree with me. After all, I set the stage by distancing myself from Hunter. Anger or impassivity would be expected—welcome even. He didn't display either.

"If I take that back, it won't change anything," he said calmly. "I will always love you, Izzie. You have my heart. How are you going to return that?"

"You don't get it."

He took the ring and slipped it back on my finger. "Oh, but I do. I've heard your thoughts. I've felt your anxiety. Marriage is a serious endeavor.

If I had issues with infidelity, I could have married and divorced several times. Plenty of females have thrown themselves at me, wanting to tie the knot. I refused every one of them, looking for my soul mate. You."

"Nice words, Hunter. What happens when you tire of me?"

He cupped my face between his hands. "Will never happen. I promise you that. I also promise you that we're having this out with Nita. She's influenced you for years without even realizing it. She won't continue to do this."

Hunter gave me a quick kiss and stood.

"Where are you going?"

"Going to call Whisper Falls Inn. It's time that your mother moved out."

When I came out of the shower, Hunter was gone. I dressed and went down to the great room, waiting for his return. Mom made herself a sandwich and joined me.

"You're alone?" She sat on the sofa.

"For now. Hunter had business to—"

Mom smirked. "And so it begins."

Before I could reply, Hunter entered the room. "That's enough!"

We both looked up. Mom set her plate on the table and frowned. "I was waiting for this."

"What are you talking about, Mom?"

She leaned into the pillows. "Your future husband doesn't like my speaking the truth. He's afraid I'll talk you out of marrying him."

What a joke. "Kind of too late for that, Mom. I already called it off."

What happened next was surprisingly sad. Instead of Mom showing her dismay or sorrow, she grinned. "I guess you learned from me after all. You're better off without him. We can get our own place, Izzie."

Hunter laughed. "You're so predictable. My grandfather warned me about you." My former fiancé glanced over at me. "I didn't tell you because I didn't want to upset you, but Baba had another vision. He saw how this woman was driving a wedge between us, and if I didn't stop it, we'd end up by ourselves and miserable. The only one who would benefit from the situation would be her."

My jaw dropped.

Mom, however, shook her head. "Damn shamans. They're always butting in where they're not wanted."

Hunter walked toward Mom. He stopped in front of the coffee table. "Would you like me to tell the rest of your story?"

She rolled her eyes and waved her hand. Shoving to her feet, she said, "It doesn't matter. I'm out of here. Stupid of me to think that my daughter would want to help me out."

I was lost. Did Hunter know something I didn't? "What's going on?"

Baba came into the room and cut off my mother's departure. "This woman is not who she claims to be."

"Huh?" I said as I stood.

"She is not your mother, but your aunt," Baba said. "Tell your niece the truth. She deserves it."

My gaze bounced around the room. "Somebody better tell me something."

The woman I'd called Mom crossed her arms over her chest and kept her mouth closed. Hunter gave me a downturned expression. It was Baba who finally spoke up.

"After Hunter told me what your aunt claimed to happen to her, I took a quest. The ancestors allowed me to speak to your mother. She died in that car accident. According to her, she took her eyes off the road when her phone rang."

Slowly, I sat down. "What else did Mom say?"

"She told me about your aunt, Arleta. You never knew your mother had a twin," Baba said.

Facing the woman, I asked, "Was any of your story true?"

"Yes. I got involved with someone bad for me. I simply wanted to start over."

"How did you know where to find me?"

Arleta's eyebrows knitted together for a moment. "You knew a man named Kazimir Chekhov. His brother is Ivan, the person I was involved with. Ivan claimed that Kazimir tracked you to Colorado. I went to my own shaman, who clued me in on the general area. He couldn't be sure where you were, though. I took my chances running from Ivan. Just dumb luck that our paths crossed."

Coincidence or not, I didn't like it. Would others come looking for me?

Hunter tugged at my elbow. "Let's talk outside."

Closing the door behind him, he stared at me before saying, "I felt your fear, but there's nothing to worry about. I went to see Addie after speaking to Baba. We came up with a plan."

"What is it?"

"I told you I'd involve SIN—well, Liam's in on it. He'll help transport your aunt to Denver. Once she leaves town, her memory of Havenwood Falls will erase. She won't remember seeing you or even speaking to this shaman either."

I nodded. "That's good. Why did she lie to me?"

Hunter moved closer and pulled me into an embrace. "I had Monte look into Arleta's story. He found evidence of Ivan Chekhov. That man is more despicable than his brother ever was."

"How so?"

"He runs a sex-for-hire trade. A woman matching Arleta's description has been missing for about a week."

My eyes widened. "She won't be safe."

"Yes, she will. We'll change Arleta's appearance before she leaves. The plan is to get her on a plane headed out of the country."

Part of me wanted to keep her in Havenwood Falls, but like Senora pointed out—I couldn't trust my aunt.

After Hunter left with Arleta, I began preparing dinner. When I closed the fridge door, Senora was standing on the other side. She wore her usual snug-fitting jeans, red leather jacket, and stilettos.

"Not sticking around for dinner?" I asked.

"Not unless you're serving my steak raw." She sauntered over to a stool at the island. "I'm still trying to get used to eating road kill."

Laughing, I said, "It's not that bad. Give it time. You might find yourself craving burgers."

She shuddered. "How are you doing?"

I shrugged. "It's a lot to take in. Arleta brought back the memories I thought I'd squashed."

"There's nothing wrong with remembering, Izzie. It's what you do with those thoughts that matters."

"Perhaps." I considered Senora's words as I seasoned the steaks.

"I heard you were calling off the engagement."

"Senora—"

"Want my advice?"

I knew her long enough to know that the advice was coming whether or not I wanted it.

"If you let Arleta influence you, she wins." Senora held up her hand. "Hunter loves you and is totally devoted to you. He went out of his way to prove your aunt's story. He's keeping her safe to give you peace of mind. Does that sound like a man who will dump you when the going gets rough?"

No, it didn't.

"That's what I've been trying to tell her." Hunter gave Senora's shoulder a squeeze before coming over to me. "Problem is, I don't know how to get her to believe it."

"I believe you," I said. Getting Hunter to believe me was the new issue.

He quirked an eyebrow, gave me a quick kiss, and said, "I've got church tonight. Don't wait up."

My heart sunk. Meetings with the MC could run late. "I guess there's no need to fix dinner."

After Hunter left the kitchen, Senora came over and took the pepper mill from my hand. "Skip this. We'll go out."

I stood there like an idiot with spices and blood dripping from my hands. "Where?"

"Let's swing by Silk. Have a girls' night out."

Ignoring her suggestion, I moved to the sink and washed up. "I think I might have blown it with Hunter."

Senora sighed. "Then fix it. You told him that you didn't want to get married. He didn't believe you. Now you're upset that he doubts your feelings for him? Seriously, girlfriend, get a fucking clue."

Drying my hands, I faced her. "And what clue would that be?"

"Actions speak louder than words. You've been dragging your ass around here ever since Arleta came to town. Are you going to let her screw up a good thing?"

"No." Despite my apprehension, meeting Hunter really was a blessing. He knew me inside and out in every way possible. My past—in the form of words from Mom and Arleta—was holding me back, and it had to stop. "Question is what do I do?"

"Do you still want to marry Hunter?"

The answer lay on the tip of my tongue, but I didn't want to rush it. After all, there might be a good reason not to marry him.

"Izzie, listen to your heart," Senora urged. "It will never steer you wrong."

For once, I followed advice. I shut my eyes and connected with my beast. She wanted Hunter. She trusted him, and I was willing to trust her. When I looked at my best friend, I knew exactly what I had to do.

❄

All around Havenwood Falls, residents were preparing for the night's festivities—Cupids & Cuties and the Sweetheart Dance at the high school. If my life had turned out differently, maybe I would have wanted to take part, but I'd never been a fan of PDA. Possibly it had more to do with my parents' marriage falling apart and less with any type of preference. It didn't matter. I had a different type of celebration in mind for Hunter.

When Senora and I told Baba the plan, he volunteered his services. Everything was set at the cabin—decorations were in place, food was ready, and there was lots of champagne on ice. The hardest part was getting the key members of SIN on board. Thankfully, Liam talked to Melaina and the dancers from Silk were coming, too.

My hand shook as I touched the wine-colored strapless dress. On such short notice I was fortunate to find something suitable at Callie's Consignment shop. Delicate roses trimmed the full skirt while the bodice sported a delicate embroidered pattern. A pair of silver, strappy sandals completed the outfit.

"Ready to go?" Senora asked, coming into the bedroom.

I zipped up the garment bag and said, "I think so. Did Monte pick up Hunter?"

"Yup. He used the excuse that there was an issue at his family's cabin. Plumbing or some stupid shit like that. There's a tuxedo stashed for Hunter."

"Then we'd better go. The bride can't be late."

Minutes later, we were all in place. The cabin was decked out with pink and red roses, hearts attached to ribbons hanging from the ceiling, and even white balloons. Folding chairs replaced the leather sofa and chairs. At the front of the room, anchoring everything, was a wooden platform with flowers.

My heart pounded as I waited in the shadows, holding a handmade bouquet of champagne and white ribbon roses interspersed with pearls and lace.

"Here they come," Liam shouted.

A door creaked open, and I heard his voice. "How the hell . . . What the fuck?"

Heels clicked across the floor, and then I heard Senora. "You have exactly ten minutes to get dressed. We want to get this party started."

I stifled a laugh. Hunter wasn't about to argue with her.

The first notes of Alina Baraz's "Yours" played—my cue to make that walk. Senora was beside me. "You got this."

I nodded and inched forward. Our friends watched me sashay up the aisle. The butterflies were at bay. My heart beat steadily. And my beast? She purred, contented that I'd made the right decision.

"Damn beautiful," Hunter said when I stopped beside him.

Baba cleared his throat as the music stopped. "It is my honor to perform this long-awaited ceremony. Hunter and Izzie join hands, please."

Our eyes met, and the nerves returned.

"Hunter Mitchell James, will you take Isadora Maria Itzae to be your wife, to love, honor, and cherish her now and forevermore?"

He smiled. "I will."

"Isadora Maria Itzae, will you take Hunter Mitchell James as your husband? Will you pledge to share your life openly with him, to speak the truth to him in love? Will you promise to honor and tenderly care for him, to encourage his fulfillment as an individual through all the changes in your lives?"

Honestly? Why did I have to make a bigger commitment?

Just do it, my beast urged.

I giggled and said, "I'll try to."

Everyone laughed, including Baba.

"The rings, please," he said.

Senora took my bouquet and placed the faceted band of gray titanium in my hand. I was so lucky to have her in my life. The type of ring was her idea.

I faced Hunter. He held a yellow gold ring. The filigree design with halo diamonds belonged to his mother. I'd seen the pictures.

"Izzie, this ring is a symbol of my love and faithfulness." He slipped it onto my finger. "I commit my heart and soul to you. Wear this ring as a reminder of the vows we've made."

Swallowing hard, I said, "Hunter, I give you this ring to wear with love and joy. A ring has no end and neither does my love for you. I pledge to you all that I am and all that I will ever be as your wife."

When I stood there not moving, Senora nudged my shoulder, prompting me to put the ring on Hunter's finger.

"Under the powers bestowed upon me by the gods and the State of Colorado, I pronounce you married. You may kiss the bride."

As Hunter's lips claimed mine, my beast gave me a silent high-five. Senora was right. Listening to my animal spirit would always guide me right, leading me home.

If you haven't already, read Hunter and Izzie's story in *Taming the Beast* by Nadirah Foxx and more about Senora in *The Collector: Awakening* by Kristie Cook, R.K. Ryals, Belinda Boring & Nadirah Foxx.

HALLOWEEN 2019

BEAUTY IN THE DARK

BY KRISTIE COOK

A Knight Twins Short Story

I hurried up the stairwell, following its spiral twist up to the top floor of Modi Tower, our home away from home here at Sun & Moon Academy's Halvard Campus. Halloween—Samhain to many and a religious holiday to some—meant classes were out until Monday. The majority of students had already left campus for the four-day weekend, causing an unusual quiet to drift through the empty spaces of the tower. My twin, Brielle, and our best friend, Charleigh, who were also my roommates, didn't really have anywhere to go, so we stayed on campus. We did plan to go to town this evening for the Haunting on Main Street, though. And, hopefully, find a party or two. My heart picked up a little speed and my steps bounced a bit higher at the thought of getting out of here. Brie and I both needed the distraction.

Halloween was our dad's birthday, and he was literally worlds away —in a completely different, alternate universe, actually. We'd come to Havenwood Falls and this version of Earth through a gate between dimensions, and our parents left us here as a safe place from all of those in our world who wanted to kill us or use us for our power. My sister and I were an anomaly—anointed angels by the Heavenly Host itself, but with the DNA of all supernatural creatures of our world, including demons. We weren't supposed to exist, our powers were unlike anyone else's and our potential unknown. Our older brother was the closest to us, but even he was different. Although this world was quite a bit nicer than our own war-ravaged one, I missed my dad terribly. And our aunts and uncles and everyone else. Sometimes even my mom, although I hadn't been able to forgive her for what she'd done right before we came here.

But that wasn't the only thing stirring within me. Ever since that whole event with Taylor Augustine and the spirits over a month ago, a heaviness had been growing. The sensation was familiar but unwanted. Something else we'd been hiding from, hoping it wouldn't find us here in this dimension. But it had. Of course it had.

After all, the Darkness was a part of my sister and me.

Drawn to us, especially me. Or I was drawn to it. That seemed to be the consensus among those who knew, and I honestly couldn't deny it. Brielle hated it, but I found something comforting about the Dark energy when it swirled within me. It was one reason I had a hard time forgiving my mom. Brie and Charleigh said I needed to, for myself, because resentment only fed that Darkness. They just didn't understand that the Darkness and I were old friends, and I didn't mind feeding her.

She gave me the feeling of belonging, of home. Not our home world, but another one Brie and I had unintentionally opened a gate to when we were young. A much, much Darker world, overtaken by evil. The heady sensation coursed through my blood, feeding my powers. But I knew how dangerous they could be. If I unleashed my powers—or worse, lost control—we'd surely be kicked out of SMA and Havenwood Falls altogether. And then what? I didn't want to know. With the veil between worlds at its thinnest tonight, the Darkness may feel even stronger, its call louder, and I needed to find a way to ignore it, even when part of me longed to embrace it. To embrace her.

So yeah, a distraction in town was exactly what I needed tonight.

When I reached the top of the stairwell that spiraled up the center of Modi Tower, I found a scattering of something black at the doorway to our floor.

"What the hell?" I wondered aloud as I bent to touch one. Soft and velvety—rose petals. I quickly realized they weren't scattered randomly, as though blown in by the wind. They created a trail that curved with the walls right to our dorm room. "Brie? Charleigh?" I called out to them, but nobody answered.

I halted at the door. It was shut, and hovering at eye level in front of it was a black rose with a long black stem, a silver note tied to it:

Elliana, I see you—your strength, your softness when you think no one is looking, and yes, your thorns, too.

I didn't recognize the handwriting. It wasn't Brie's or Charleigh's, and the note was obviously meant for me, considering my name was on it. As I glanced around, scenting the air for any clues, a thrill ran through me. All I could sense was magic—not my sister's or my best friend's, though closer to Brie's than Charleigh's witch powers. Fae magic, maybe.

Plucking the rose out of the air, I fingered the note. The lettering changed.

I want you to see me. I want you to know. Come to where the magic swirls and the night sky awaits.

With a quiet snort, I shook my head as I entered the room. It had to be some guy, probably patting himself on the back for thinking he was so romantic. The thing was, I wasn't into guys. They did nothing for me. The luscious curves of the right woman's body, though . . . the soft press of her full lips against mine . . . just the thought could make my knees weak and my heart flutter.

I'd finally found her—the right woman—in our home world, but I was pretty sure she'd never have anything to do with me, especially now, since I'd left when she needed me most. And now, with a new war probably started, I didn't even know if she was still alive. I'd been trying my best to let go. Destiny had been a distraction at the beginning of the semester, but nothing ever happened with us. She had her eyes on someone else. There was one other girl here who'd caught my attention, but I was pretty sure she was straight.

I hated to encourage my secret admirer—guys didn't always react too well when I told them their junk was all wrong for me. Not that I put it that way. Well, I did once, but the asshat thought he could change my mind, that he was the one who would make me go straight. *Puh-lease*. So insulting his man parts was the only way to get him off my back—literally. I shuddered at the memory of his erection pressing against my ass. *Gross*.

Dropping the rose on my dresser, I pulled out the pieces of my costume. Charleigh, who was not only our best friend and cousin but also our protector, approved of my choice since it included wearing my fighting leathers from home, specially enchanted for extra protection. I quickly dressed in the black leather pants, corset, and knee-high stiletto heeled boots. A flutter of my hand over my head glamoured my dark hair into black horns and my makeup to look just right. Adorning the cape with the huge collar, I stepped in front of the full-length mirror and admired my version of Maleficent.

"Wow! You look great!" my twin said from behind me. She kicked the door shut before coming over and doing a slow walk around me, then held out a cup with Coffee Haven's logo on it. "A special Halloween treat. Roxy called it Scream Like a Ghoul—it's got a cinnamon kick to it. I thought you'd like it since you like to make girls scream."

She gave me a teasing grin.

"Haha." I took the drink from her and sipped at the warm concoction. "Mmm . . . not bad. Now hurry up and get ready!"

Brielle pulled a face. "I think I'm going to stay here. It's so peaceful."

Narrowing my eyes, I shook my head and waved a finger at her. "Hell, no! Not tonight, Brielle Sophia Ames Knight. You are coming to town with us, and we're going to have *fun*."

"But I really need to study."

"Bullshit. You have all weekend to study. Besides, what do you need to study? Your memory is nearly perfect."

She shrugged. "Stuff."

I crossed my arms over my chest and jutted out my hip. "Now I know you're definitely full of bullshit. You're hiding here. But you know we shouldn't be alone tonight. Come to town with me. We'll watch the parade and get a cupcake to celebrate Dad's birthday. Then we'll go from there."

She frowned, but when she pulled her bottom lip between her teeth, I knew I had her. "Okay, fine. But no promises after that."

"Yay!" I clapped my hands together. "Get your costume on. What are you going to be anyway? And where the hell is Charleigh?"

"She went to town early to scope everything out and make sure it was safe. And I wasn't really planning on dressing as anything. I could just throw my leathers on and be Elliana Knight."

I lifted an eyebrow. "First of all, you wouldn't really look any different—though maybe hotter." I winked at her, and she rolled her eyes. "Second, why the hell would you want to be me? And third, being me means you can't pick up guys!"

"I wouldn't just be you. I'd be future you—Elliana Knight, elite demon assassin."

A grin stretched across my face. I couldn't wait to become exactly that, whenever we got back to our own world. It was what I was training for here at SMA, though I couldn't really tell anyone else, since the demons in this world were quite a bit different. Less Hellish and more human-like, at least on the surface. Some were even tolerable, as though their time among the humans here had caused them to evolve. Quite the opposite of our world, where they were nothing but evil. I had this belief that if we could rid our world of all of them, the Darkness would be gone for good, too—the dangerous temptress removed from my life once and for all. Maybe everyone would then stop treating me the way they did.

"I like the sound of that," I said. "Okay, demon assassin, hurry up and get dressed. We need to get our party on!"

"Fine," she said with an exasperated sigh. "Go meet Charleigh at the fountain before she comes all the way back to the room. I'll be there in a few."

"I'm not leaving here without you." I dropped my hands to my hips and cocked my head. "Because I know you—you'll never come."

"I promise I'll be there in ten minutes."

My eyes narrowed again. "Pinky swear?"

She held up her hand, pinky out. "*Twin* pinky swear."

We curled our pinky fingers around each other's and shook. She couldn't go back on a twin swear. That was one thing we'd never do to each other, even with something as trivial as a night out.

As a last minute thought, I grabbed the black rose on my way out the door. I didn't know what I was going to do with it, but maybe I could make it part of my costume.

The campus was eerily quiet as I crossed it. The light coming in from the skylight above was dim, meaning it was nearing dusk outside. I hated to encourage whoever left the beautiful black rose, but I really didn't have a choice but to go to the portals—where the magic swirled —because it was the only way out. I hurried for them, mentally bracing myself in case he was there, but still excited to be outside and free for a while.

After growing up in a nuclear shelter for the majority of my life, I'd had enough of living underground, thank you very much. But here we were, living in a mountain. We didn't have it as bad as some of the students who weren't used to it, like we were, but I could understand how they felt. Once we'd adjusted to life above ground—and protected ourselves against all the dangers in our world—the freedom of just being able to step outside right out of your home and feel the sunshine on your skin or see the moon from your window, to run or fly without boundaries, became intoxicating. Being underground again sometimes felt suppressing and stifling.

A twelve-foot Valkyrie statue stood in the center of the vestibule where the portals were, a purple flame in her lifted palm providing the only light, but just enough to illuminate more black petals scattered in front of the three archways of the portals. Another long-stemmed black rose hovered in front of the center arch, with another note tied to it.

Elliana, There is beauty even in darkness, it can't be denied. Like these black roses, I see it in you. Come to the fountain where the water flows.

I looked around, smelled the air. Nobody was in sight, and all I could smell was the magic of the portals, overpowering any traces of the magic holding the rose in midair. I didn't even have that sense of being watched, but how did he know I'd be the one to find this rose?

"Whatever," I muttered to myself, plucking the flower out of the air and using magic to sweep up the petals. Whoever this dude was, he was going to be severely disappointed. I almost felt bad for him. But then again, he should have known already, if he'd been paying attention at all. That was the thing about most guys, though—they rarely did pay attention, nuances and subtleties often lost on them.

I had a passing thought that maybe we could be friends, at least, but I didn't need another "friend." Especially not in this world. We wouldn't be here forever, after all. I also considered introducing him to my twin, but I was pretty sure Aithan Lanrete would be the one to win her over, if she ever gave him the chance. So far, she was completely oblivious to his interest, no matter how many times Charleigh and I tried to convince her otherwise.

Right before I stepped through the portal, I snapped my wings out, something I wouldn't be able to do once in town. While we were free to use our powers and abilities on the SMA campus, it was forbidden outside, where norms—normal humans, which our parents called normans, but we shortened to norms—lived unaware that their hometown was populated by supernaturals. The top two rules in Havenwood Falls were *bring no harm to humans* and *protect the secret.* I glamoured my normally purple and black feathers to be completely black and to look less real than they were, making them part of my costume and completing the look of Maleficent. I'd just have to be very careful to not move them as though they were a natural part of my body.

The magic rippled over me as I passed through the portal, stepping out on the other side in a room at the Falls Campus of the lower school of Sun and Moon Academy. Following the path to the main part of the private school for the town's supernatural kids, I came to the courtyard with the fountain at its center. Again, I didn't have a choice of coming to where the water flows. This was where I was supposed to meet Charleigh and wait for Brielle.

Charleigh wasn't there yet, and overcome with intrigue, I couldn't help but walk around the fountain, searching for my secret admirer. He was nowhere to be seen or sensed, though. No trace of him anywhere.

However, there was the bright orange hair of my best friend since we were babies—besides Brielle, of course—cousin, in a way, and sworn protector. Sworn to my mother, matriarch of the society that was leading our Earth back to civilization. Or it was trying to, anyway. But that's another story. The short of it was we were basically considered royalty at home, and our kind always had a sworn protector. As a witch with powers that rivaled any sorceress, Charleigh was ours. It allowed her to come to this world with us.

"Where's Brielle?" she asked as she strode into the courtyard, dressed as a medieval bar wench.

"She said she'll be right here."

Stopping in front of me, she dropped a hand to her waist. "You just left her, Elli? You know she'll never come now!"

"She twin swore," I said confidently. "Brielle will not go back on that."

Blowing out an exasperated breath, she nodded. "If she's not here in five minutes, I'm going after her."

I clapped a hand to my chest, widened my eyes, and took on my best damsel-in-distress voice, Southern accent and all. "And leave me all alone out here in this big world without a protector? But how will I ever cope?"

For an extra scoop of dramatic flair, I dropped my head back and pressed the back of my hand to my forehead.

Charleigh smirked. "You can't pull that shit off as Elliana Knight, but especially not as Maleficent. I have a feeling you'd be just fine, especially in this town."

"Damn right, I would be," I said, straightening up and grinning. "So why the need to come do a pre-check for our safety?"

She crossed her arms over her chest. "Because sometimes I like to feel useful. At least feel like I'm *trying* to do my job." She lifted a hand and gave a dismissive wave. "Of course, everything is fine. Whatever threats lurk, we can surely handle."

"What did you expect?"

"*However*," she continued, ignoring my question, "the veil is thinnest tonight, and we know that could cause . . . certain problems. We all stick together tonight. Understood?"

I gave her a salute. "Yes, sir!"

Rolling her eyes, she laughed. "Again, it just doesn't come off right when you're dressed as the Evil Queen herself. As if I needed another reason not to trust you."

"As if you aren't her favorite partner in crime," Brielle teased from the archway leading into the courtyard.

Charleigh's brows furrowed as she studied my sister. "You didn't dress up? It's Halloween!"

"But I did. I'm Elliana Knight, demon assassin." She did a little spin on *my* heeled-boots. One of my other pairs of knee-high black boots. What can I say? A girl could never have too many pairs of shoes or boots. With her black leather pants, dark purple bustier, loose curls tumbling down her back, her makeup fierce, and wings out, she looked like a perfect duplicate of me. You'd think that'd be easy for her, since we're identical twins, but our styles were so different, we rarely ever looked exactly alike anymore.

"Damn, I'm hot!" I proclaimed. "You look amazing!"

"Let's go," Charleigh said, looping her arms into each of ours. "The parade will start soon, and we want a good spot."

Arm in arm, we headed out of the courtyard and toward the real world. Well, if you could call Havenwood Falls the real world, which it was as far away from as you could possibly get. But at least we were free from the confines of the mountain. I inhaled the crisp, fresh air and took in the beautiful sight of the peaks surrounding us. I liked mountains—the *outsides* of them—and this box canyon was definitely picturesque.

Sensing something behind us, I glanced over my shoulder and stopped in my tracks. Another black rose lay on the edge of the fountain's bowl. But there was nobody around.

"What the hell, Elli?" Charleigh asked when I pulled both of them to a stop.

I broke free of her hold. "You two go ahead. I'll catch up."

"What did you just promise not five minutes ago?"

I didn't answer, rushing back over to the fountain. Snatching the rose up, I quickly read the note tied to it.

Not this fountain. The one that sparkles, even in the dark, much like you.

"What's with the roses?" Brielle asked when I rejoined them, noticing for the first time the three I now held.

"Some secret admirer," I said dismissively, but then I laughed. "Be prepared, Brie. He might think you're me! Maybe you'll actually get some tonight."

Charleigh laughed, but Brielle only snorted. "The only thing I'll get is to let him down nicely without insulting his man parts."

"But then you wouldn't be me," I pointed out.

"Oh, right." She cleared her throat, lifted her chest and her chin so she looked down on us, and mimicked my voice. "Dude, not that I can really feel the little, half-flaccid lump between your legs that you're trying to grind against me, but if you do it one more time, I'll rip it off and feed it to the dogs who must have raised you."

Charleigh laughed again. "I still can't believe you did that, Elli, but it was classic."

"He deserved it, even if I were straight," I reminded her.

"Damn right," they both agreed. I hadn't been the only one he'd harassed. He thought that thing between his legs was God's gift to the world and all women should bow down and worship it. For the second time in an hour, I shuddered at the memory.

We made our way to Main Street and toward town square, marveling at all of the Halloween decorations. We'd never seen anything like it—such things didn't exist in our world. Our parents had told us about how beautiful homes and shops used to be at Christmastime in the Before time (the time before the War of Armageddon). Greenery, which we didn't have much of anymore even in nature, red ribbons, silver and gold bulbs, and lights of all colors would make the world extra-magical, they said. But they'd never mentioned people doing the same for Halloween.

"They must make a bigger deal of this holiday than our world ever did," I said as we found a spot on the edge of Town Square Park.

"Based on my research, this isn't quite normal," Brie said. "This town goes all out, compared to other places. But no other place has a population like the one here. It's a true holiday here."

She was careful about how she said it, with norms surrounding us.

The parade was mostly kids showing off their costumes, but even those weren't like the ones we'd seen on TV, all plastic and weird masks. They were elaborate and fun, some so good that I had to wonder if glamour or witch magic played a role in creating them. After it was over, the crowd quickly dispersed. Parents took the kids trick-or-treating at the businesses and throughout the residential neighborhoods.

"According to Dillys, there's a bonfire party by the lake in Danzan Park," Charleigh said. "If Natalie and Tempest are there, we'll surely be concocting some amazing drinks."

"I saw them leave," Brielle said. "Right after the parade ended. With Micah, the angel."

Another difference between our worlds: Angels walked the earth here. Micah wasn't the only one. An angel named Cece ran the music store in town, and there were others, in town and out. The only angels who walked the earth in our world were our kind—my mother's bloodline, deemed Earth's Angels by the Heavenly Host in the Otherworld. I had so many questions about that, but hadn't sought answers. While Micah was on campus a lot, he was a bit intimidating.

"Oh, that's strange. I know how much they were looking forward to tonight." Charleigh shrugged and gave me a devious grin. "I guess it's up to us to create the fun and mischief."

My lips quirked up. "Oh, we can definitely do that."

Brielle groaned. "I think that's my cue to head back to campus."

"NO!" Charleigh and I said together.

"I won't allow it," Charleigh said, claiming my twin's arm with her own, as though she planned to hang on to her all night if she had to. "You need this break, whether you think you do or not."

"Okay, fine." Brie gave an exaggerated sigh. "Since I'm already out here . . . But I swear, if we end up in jail, I promise you will wake up under a pile of snow every day for the rest of the semester." She wriggled her fingers, though she didn't produce the ice crystals she was capable of. She knew better than to do so in town. We both could manipulate the elements, though she was better with water and earth while I was stronger with fire and air.

We started down the sidewalk that cut through Town Square Park. Night had completely fallen, and the whole area was lit up by orange, neon green, and purple lights in the trees, around the lamp posts, and in many shop windows. Other shops were lit with black lights illuminating their neon displays in a trippy way. The whole thing was trippy for me, though. Although we'd been in this world since last spring, we still weren't used to all the lights and electricity, especially used in such lavish ways as colored lights solely for the purpose of decoration. We had electricity at home, but it was limited. Every time they tried to build a more widespread power grid, the whole thing fried from the black magic still lingering since the big war. Or it'd be wiped out by the many (un)natural disasters.

I knew Brielle was trying to learn how to fix that while we were here in this world, but I just didn't see how. Magic and the supernatural were still in hiding here—suppressed, contained, silenced

—and they *still* had some issues with interference, especially in a town like Havenwood Falls, where the magic was so dominant. Our campus was even worse. Candles and fires were used more often than electric lights, and the tech stuff was always hit-or-miss, except in Haldor Hall, which was specifically insulated from the effects of magic. If they still had all these problems here, how did Brielle think she could do anything in our world, where magic was rampant, especially of the black kind?

But that was her thing, not mine. She was incredibly intelligent when it came to that stuff, much like our dad. My strengths lay elsewhere. Also like my dad, who was good at pretty much everything.

As we approached the fountain, I slowed, trailing behind Brie and Charleigh as they gave it a wide berth, cutting across the center part of the park. The gold flakes that were inlaid into the basin glinted from the colorful lights, catching my eye. *The one that sparkles, even in the dark, just like you.* I edged closer, curiosity once again gripping me. A thrill ran through me when I spotted the black rose laying on the fountain's edge, with another note tied to it:

Elliana, Like fire and water, earth and air, I see in you the forces of both creation and destruction. Beautiful, dangerous, compelling. Come to where the four meet.

Okay, that one was sort of weird, though if I had to admit it, in a kind of flattering way. Snatching it up, more so nobody else would see it than wanting to keep it, I hurried to catch up to Brielle and Charleigh. My gaze swept the area, and I sent my senses out, trying to pinpoint the culprit, but the few people still in the square had no interest in me or the rose, immersed in their own activities.

"Another one?" Charleigh asked. Her hand snaked out and grabbed the growing bunch from my grip. Without faltering in her steps, she quickly read through the notes. "Wow, he really does have it bad. I kind of feel sorry for the poor sap. I do think Brielle should take this one on."

"Hey! First of all, I don't want or need Elli's rejects," Brie said indignantly. "That said, I feel bad for him, too, considering how much trouble he's gone through and your history with guys, El. Maybe I *should* be the one to tell him the truth."

"You sure you don't want him?" I teased. "He does seem quite the romantic. Everything he's said so far applies to you, too. Maybe you'll hit it off."

"Absolutely not," Brie answered.

"Besides, she already has her own admirer, if she'd just open her eyes," Charleigh said, elbowing my twin in the ribs. She dropped her voice to a whisper. "Don't look now, but Aithan Lanrete is about half a block behind us. He's been nearby, but at a distance all evening. Maybe tonight's the night!"

"Or maybe he's *Elli's* secret admirer," Brie suggested.

Charleigh laughed. "Naw, not his style. If he were to get all romantic, he'd write a song and serenade."

"The night's still young," Brie replied. "Maybe that's at the end point."

She just didn't get it. He was so into her, and she was completely oblivious. At least he wasn't a total creeper, which I was beginning to wonder if my admirer was. But I had to think about it objectively—if it were a girl I was interested in, would I feel the same way? Or would I be impressed? That thrill ran through me again, making my stomach flutter. Okay, I admit I'd be impressed, or, at least, a little excited.

I didn't understand the last instructions until we finally reached the lake at Danzan Park. A bonfire was already blazing on the sandy beach near the water, flames reaching high into the air—where the four elements met.

As we went to the table offering a brew of Mountain Dew Me, the school's signature drink Charleigh and the other witches had created, I expected my secret admirer to approach. I mean, here I was, where the four elements met. Was he going to chicken out now? It would make my life easier, not having to let him down, but the curiosity just might kill me. In fact, the longer I waited, the more it was bugging me, and thoughts about how to teach this dude a lesson—not in a nice way—started swirling.

"Brie's gotta pee," Charleigh said after handing me a cup. "Coming with us?"

I shook my head. "I'll stay here by the fire." Her lips pulled to the side as she studied the area, so I added, "I'll be fine for a few minutes. There's too many people here—future guardians, at that—for anything to happen. And even if it did, we're still well within the town's wards. The Court and coven would be here instantly."

She sighed. "Okay, but you stay right here. Promise me."

I nudged her. "Just go. And relax or you're going to ruin our fun."

She blew out another breath, this was one harder, before smiling. "Yeah, you're right. Sorry. I don't know what's gotten into me."

Taking Brie's arm again, they hurried off toward the concession stand and bathrooms. I remained by the bonfire, sipping my brew and pretending to watch the flames while taking in the surroundings. It was a beautiful scene—snow-capped mountains rising around us, the calm lake reflecting the millions of stars in the sky, the flames dancing on the beach . . .

Something caught my attention off to the right, and I turned my head for a better view. Another fire started closer to where the forest met the beach. A lone figure stood there, and I could almost feel him beckoning me. Glancing around to see if anyone else noticed—no, they didn't—I made my way over there.

Maybe I was being stupid. Maybe this was a trap. Maybe Charleigh was going to murder me if this guy didn't kill me or sweep me back to our world—or worse, that Dark one we'd opened the gate to. But I didn't feel Darkness as I approached. I didn't sense any kind of nefarious energy. In fact, it was the quite opposite—light, hope, warmth.

And the figure was not a he.

Although she wore a cloak so I couldn't see the dress from a distance, I saw now shapely legs and the curve of her breasts in her silhouette against the fire she'd built. When she turned toward me, holding out a skull with a black rose between its teeth, I gasped. Under the mask that only covered the upper part of her face, her full red lips curled up as I came closer. Her long white hair was pulled into a braid that spilled over one shoulder, peeking out from the cloak's hood. When her electric blue eyes caught mine, my breath caught and my heart went erratic.

"You?" I whispered.

She stepped up to me, only inches away. "I was afraid you wouldn't come. But I'm so glad you did."

She tilted her head, leaned forward, and pressed her luscious lips against mine—softly, cautiously. A shockwave racked through my body. I couldn't believe this was happening. I'd been eyeing her all semester, but I never expected this. When she started to pull back, I slid my hands over her jaw and into her hair, bringing her closer as I deepened the kiss. She tasted even better than I'd ever imagined, and I'd been imagining this way more than I ever realized until now.

When we broke apart, her hand found mine and squeezed. I glanced over my shoulder, toward the party, and saw the two familiar figures coming closer. I knew it wouldn't take them long to find me.

"You want to go back to the party?"

Her lips curved into a small smile, but she shook her head. "I can't right now. But I wanted you to know."

She leaned up again as her hand snaked around my neck, bringing me in for another knee-weakening kiss, her lips parting and her tongue darting in, but only briefly. Just enough for a taste.

And then she was gone.

My heart continued racing, but my stomach sank at her quick departure. What the hell?

"Who was that?" Brie asked.

I swallowed, unable to bring myself to say, even to my twin. For some reason, I wanted to keep this to myself, keep the magical moment as my own, if just for a little while. "Um . . . just my secret admirer. Not so secret now. But don't worry. I let him down easy."

"So who was it?" Charleigh asked.

"A guy from my Critical Thinking class. I don't think you know him."

She shrugged. "Well, then, can we get our party on now?"

"Definitely." As we headed back to the big fire and the rest of the party, I glanced over my shoulder. She was nowhere to be seen, disappeared into the night.

I just wanted you to know. Now I did know. A final thrill ran through me at the thought of our kiss, and I vowed it would not be the last one.

Read about the Knight twins in *Sun & Moon Academy Book One: Fall Semester* and *Sun & Moon Academy Book Two: Spring Semester* (coming Spring 2020).

HOLIDAY SEASON 2019

(UN)GRATEFUL BASTARD

BY KRISTIE COOK

An Addie Beaumont Short Story

*H*eat poured out of the oven as I inspected my first-ever Thanksgiving turkey, basting it, wiggling the legs, and checking the thermometer one more time. It looked pretty damn good, if I did say so myself—golden herbed skin, clear juices leaking—and the smell. Mouthwatering! I'd been dreaming about turkey and mashed potatoes and gravy and stuffing for weeks, and I didn't care what that said about me.

"Adelaide, it smells wonderful and looks perfect," my grandmother said as I pulled the bird out and sat it on the granite counter of her massive kitchen. "Might I say even better than Chef's? But don't tell her that."

She gave me a wink—as uncharacteristic as the jeans and green sweater she wore and her silvery white hair flowing freely to her shoulders. You'd think I'd be used to seeing my own grandma dressed casually, but Saundra Beaumont was never seen outside her home without her pressed business suit and her hair pulled up in a French twist. And since I'd never felt at home in the Beaumont estate, I wasn't here often.

"Thank you, Grandmother. Now, I just have to get everything else done. Dinner will be ready . . . soon." I glanced at the clock: four-thirty. Technically, it should be ready right on the dot at five o'clock, but I didn't want to be so specific, in case I had to dawdle a bit longer to give Tase time to arrive. He was supposed to be here hours ago, helping me.

We thought our first Thanksgiving together as an actual couple—and not our prior on-again-off-again status—we'd cook for our families. Well, my family. His, the Rocas, refused to set foot in the Beaumont estate. Besides, they were eating at Whisper Falls Inn with their other big brother, Xandru, and Michaela. Although the Beaumont side wasn't big, I just couldn't see inviting everyone to my little home with its tiny kitchen. Not when Grandmother had this professional chef's kitchen with plenty of room to maneuver. And dude, did I need it! Even without Tase's promised help, I couldn't imagine trying to make all these dishes in cramped quarters.

Besides, we needed the buffer. Things had been not so great between Tase and me. Perhaps we were never meant to be an actual couple. He'd proposed last New Year's Eve. Even though I'd loved him since I was fourteen years old, I never gave him a direct answer. How could I when his five-year-old kid—the one he'd known about for barely more than a year—had only hours earlier been dropped in his lap because the baby mama had vanished? That's what the babysitter said, anyway, and I supposed that was one way to put it. But we knew my sister and my boyfriend's ex, Rachelle, was dead, a casualty of the battle against the Collector last year.

So no, I couldn't quite take the proposal seriously. I had to know Tase wasn't just looking for a mother for his kid. That he really wanted *us*—him and me and not an instant family. Our past was too rocky. I didn't want our future to be, too. So I told him to ask me again later. And he did—a couple of times—but I kept putting off an answer. Then we each got busy and, well, it just became something I didn't want to talk about anymore, and apparently, neither did he.

It was hard to believe it'd already been nearly a year since that all went down, though. A lot had happened since, not the least of which was opening Sun & Moon Academy College of Supernatural

Guardians so our town and supernaturals around the world could better prepare for future threats like the Collector. At least she was magically trapped in a bottle and sitting in the Infernum, so she could never harm us again.

I refused to believe some of the whispers our people had heard outside of town—that the Collector still walked this earth, planning something bigger. Some of our members of the Swords of the Infernal Night—SIN Motorcycle Club—had their ears to the ground in Denver and with other chapters across the country, and SMA's Board of Regents sent out scouts to recruit students from around the world to the new college. Many had heard rumors that the Collector was not in the prison we'd given her, but nobody could prove it. We'd uncovered a couple members of her network, and they claimed she was definitely gone and they were none too happy about it. I guess she paid quite well for their unique services. So we could only assume the whispers were nothing more than rumors.

Although . . . Savage and Liam, hellhounds who often went to the underworld to escort souls there, hadn't been able to find her bottle or her soul in the Infernum. It'd either been hidden that well or . . .

I shook my head. I couldn't be thinking about such stuff right now. Today was a day to focus on family and the good things in life. Like this fabulous meal I was apparently making completely on my own.

"Hey, R2, call Asshole," I ordered my phone.

"Calling Asshole Extraordinaire on mobile," my phone's robot voice replied. A few second later, an unanswered ring repeated on the line until Tase's voicemail finally picked up.

"Where the hell are you? You were supposed to help me with this. You said it'd only take an hour when you left, and that was eight hours ago! Pick up your mother-fu—" Carter, Tase's six-year-old son and my nephew, walked into the kitchen, and I managed to break myself off and quickly correct. "Pick up your phone, Tase. Or better yet, get your butt over here."

"Yeah, Dad, get your butt over here," Carter added before I ended the call.

"Way to tell him, bud," I said.

"Aunt Addie, is dinner almost ready? I think I could eat a cow!"

"Soon. I'm trying to wait for your dad, though."

"What's taking him so long?"

"I wish I knew." I blew a loose strand of light brown hair out of my face as I glanced around the kitchen with all of the partially prepared dishes I needed to finish. "I wish I knew."

"Probably one of the lifts broke or something."

Tomorrow was opening day at the ski resort. Tase, the owner, had left early this morning to make sure everything was ready for a smooth start, including doing practice runs on the lifts and slopes, and we hadn't heard from him since. Maybe I should have gone with him. Then maybe his ass would already be here.

"Yeah, probably," I said placably, though I had to wonder if Tase was just having all the fun on the slopes by himself. I cut up some butter pats to dot on my sweet potato casserole before sliding it into one of the double ovens, wishing I was on the slopes, too, instead of trying to pretend like I was a domestic goddess or some shit—*pretend* being the operative word. What had I been thinking, anyway?

"Can I help you?" Carter asked.

I gave the mess another look. "You want to roll the crescents?"

"Sure!"

We both braced for the scary moment of when the can popped, each of us letting out a squeak when it finally did and the pale dough squished through the seam. Yeah, canned rolls, not homemade. Sue me. Like I said, I was *pretending* to be a domestic goddess. I could hold my own at home—with grilled cheese, spaghetti, mac and cheese, and the like, anyway—but truthfully, Tase was a better cook than I was. I'd never attempted such a feast as Thanksgiving dinner before, and I never would have if I'd known I'd be doing it all myself. With everything else I'd managed to prepare, canned crescent rolls would have to do.

Carter rolled the crescents as well as a six-year-old could, and maybe they weren't prime for serving at the inn or Napoli's, but I thought their imperfect shapes were just perfect.

"Thanks, dude," I said as I swept up the tray and popped it in the oven.

I checked on the other dishes I'd slid in while he rolled—an extra pan of stuffing, green bean casserole, and the sweet potatoes. Everything seemed to be coming along nicely, but it wouldn't if I delayed much longer. I let out a heavy sigh. I was going to kill that ungrateful bastard.

"Why don't you go tell Grandmother that dinner will be ready in ten minutes? Then run up to the room where I put our stuff and get your dinner clothes on," I told Carter.

"Which one? Grandma Lyra or Grandma Saundra?"

"Both."

"Okay." He ran out of the kitchen, returning a few minutes later, still wearing jeans and a T-shirt. "Joe and Fini are here."

"They are?"

He nodded. "They have been for a while."

Shit. I really did need to get everything out on the table. I was pretty sure Joe's family was expecting them at their place later.

Mom had taken Infiniti under her wing and wanted to show her that she had plenty of family here in Havenwood Falls, after all she'd been through. The girl was tougher than anyone gave her credit for, though, even herself. *Especially* herself. Perhaps throwing her into SMA right after her life had been turned upside down was too much for some, but it was probably what she needed—Joe and a distraction. For the rest of the world, her mom had been gone for over six years, but for Infiniti, it only felt like a few months. When Joe brought her to our timeline, she'd lost those six years, jumping from 2013 to 2019 in a heartbeat. She was amazingly resilient, though. And after seeing them together on campus, I knew Joe was exactly what she needed. Now that was a couple that was meant to be an actual couple.

Unlike some . . .

❄

I pounded out another text to Tase while running up the stairs to change my own clothes. By the time I returned to the kitchen, something smelled off.

"Oh, shit!" I rushed to the ovens. The marshmallows on my sweet potato casserole were quickly turning black. With a quick flick of my fingers and a few murmured words, I managed to stop the burn as I hurried to pull the dish out.

The next ten minutes consisted of a crazed dance of removing pans from the oven, orchestrating Mom, Joe, and Infiniti, who came to help carry them to the dining room (since I'd insisted Grandmother give the staff the day off), and ensuring everything was done. I went to grab the turkey to carry out the pièce de résistance when it hit me.

"Shit! The gravy! I forgot to make the gravy!"

"We have to have gravy!" Carter said, coming back into the kitchen.

"Of course we do. No worries. Tell everyone it'll be a few a more minutes." Scooping the juices out of the roasting pan, I went to work making the gravy.

A few more minutes turned into twenty more because I couldn't get the damn lumps to smooth out. At least the other dishes were sitting on warming trays in the dining room. But by the time I was done, the turkey had been sitting out for over an hour and was cold.

"Adelaide, it's rude to keep your guests waiting," Grandmother said from the kitchen doorway, now wearing her usual skirt and blouse, her hair up in its elegant chignon. "You said dinner was at five. We're approaching six now."

"I know. I'm sorry. It's done, though." I gave her a forced smile and shooed her out of the kitchen. She lifted a brow—not too many people got away with shooing Saundra Beaumont anywhere—but left.

Calling on my elemental magic of fire, boosted by my hellhound blood, I gave the turkey an extra blast of heat.

"Ack!" I nearly shouted as a flame shot out of my palm, igniting the turkey.

I must have been more worked up than I realized. A string of curse words flew out of my mouth as I quickly extinguished the fire, and more as I inspected the damage.

"My perfect turkey," I said with a devastated sigh. It was not so perfect anymore. Black spots blemished what had been beautifully golden brown skin. My fabulous feast was quickly turning into a disaster.

My heart sinking, I carried the ugly bird out to the table.

And just about dropped it when I saw Tase standing nonchalantly in the dining room, chatting with the others, holding the carving knife and fork in his hands.

Everyone stood behind their chairs at the dining table covered with an ornate brown and cream tablecloth that probably cost more than my entire dining set at home. A couple of the leaves had been removed from the usual twenty-foot table, so our small group wouldn't feel like we had to yell at each other and passing dishes would be easier. The feast was spread out among the beautiful tablescape Grandmother's staff had done, consisting of twisted branches with red berries, gourds and small pumpkins in yellow, orange, and white, pinecones, and maroon candles in shining gold candelabras. Even the crystals of the large chandelier over the table were decorated for fall.

It was a scene out of a cooking magazine—if you ignored the blackened marshmallows—but my vision had tunneled in on Tase, who gave me his signature smirk that usually made my breath catch. At the moment, I wanted to smack it right off his face.

"Need some help, Bean?" he asked, as though nothing was wrong.

Narrowing my eyes as I held his gray-green ones, I stomped over to him and practically slammed the turkey down in front of him.

"Where the hell have you been?" I hissed.

"Got held up by the lifts," he whispered. "But I'm here now. Just in time, too, it seems."

I suppressed a growl of the hellhoundish kind. "No. Just in time

71

would have been two hours ago when I needed your help in the kitchen. This was supposed to be a team effort!"

Tase glanced around the table. I could feel everyone's eyes on us, boring into the back of my head. "I'm sorry. I really am, but it was unavoidable. I'll tell you about it later, but for now, let's enjoy dinner."

I inhaled deeply through my nose, my nostrils flaring, then let it out slowly before turning and smiling as I joined everyone at the table. Instead of taking the seat next to Tase, though, I moved to the middle, across from Joe and between my mother and Carter. Grandmother sat at the head of the table on Mom's other side, her unreadable gaze following me. I could hear her silently admonishing me for my unladylike manners and lack of graciousness. Straightening my spine and squaring my shoulders, I lifted my chin and made an effort to pretend like nothing was wrong.

We all sat while Tase carved the bird, then said a blessing on the meal, giving thanks to the goddess for the food before us and the love around us. Then the dishes were passed, conversation picked up, and I began to relax. At least, from the anger. But I hadn't felt this nervous since my first day of teaching at SMA. Unable to bring myself to pick up my fork until everyone else took their first bites, I watched their faces closely.

"Uh, please pass the gravy," nearly everyone said at once.

What did that mean? Was the gravy that good, even with the lumps? They were really pouring it on now, over everything—the turkey, the stuffing, the mashed potatoes. Tentatively, I lifted a bite of turkey to my mouth.

Oh, dear goddess.

I tasted a bite of stuffing.

Oh, hell.

My mouth felt like a wad of paper and glue filled it. I took a large swallow of wine. That didn't help.

"Pass the gravy, please," I muttered.

We all ate in silence for the next few minutes. Nobody could probably speak because the paste that was supposed to be food glued their tongues to the roofs of their mouths. Everything had apparently dried out while I'd been waiting on Tase and then the gravy. My once juicy turkey was practically like leather.

"I'm so sorry," I said after suffering as long as I could. Barely a dent had been made in the food on my plate. I suppressed the threatening tears, but my voice came out thickly. "I messed up our Thanksgiving dinner!"

"No, it's really good," Joe said quickly, the awkwardness of the lie apparent on his face. Infiniti hummed in agreement next to him as she chewed on the food in her mouth—for a very long time, the forced swallow evident.

"You both are sweet, but liars," I said.

"Adelaide, don't be rude," Grandmother admonished. "These are our guests."

"Exactly. I'm not going to force them through one more moment of eating something that tastes like it was dug out of Bels Creek."

"It's . . . it's not that bad," she replied.

"It's good, honey," Mom added. "Not bad for your first feast."

"Yeah, Auntie, it's good." Carter looked up at me with a sweet smile.

"Did you use as much butter as I told you to and push it under the skin?" Tase asked.

Forks fell. Silence descended. All heads turned at once to look at Tase.

"Yes," I said through gritted teeth. Was smoke pouring out of my ears yet? "And it was perfect until it sat there for so long. *Waiting.*"

"Ah," he said. "Like the dishes out here on the warming trays? So next time you need to work on your timing."

I stared at him for a long drawn-out moment, before my lids dropped in a slow blink. Then, without even thinking about what I was doing, who was there or where we were, a piece of the crescent roll I'd been holding went flying at him, hitting his nose before landing on his plate. Everyone gasped.

"What? It's a learned skill," he said. "It takes practice to figure out the right timing for this many dishes."

"How dare you!" I yelled as I jumped up, knocking my chair over.

I chucked the rest of my roll at him, hitting him in the forehead, then grabbed whatever my fingers felt on my plate first. "You were supposed to be helping me!" I threw the handful of food at him—a piece of turkey covered in gravy. It hit his cheek, splattering across his nose and chin.

"Bean," he said quietly.

"Don't *Bean* me." I threw another handful from my plate. "This was your idea in the first place. You know I can't cook." Mashed potatoes hit his chest. "You said you'd do it! But you couldn't even bother to show up until the food was on the table!" Pieces of stuffing went flying. "And now you dare to tell me everything I did wrong! Fu—"

"Adelaide," my grandmother said quietly.

"Screw you, you ungrateful bastard! Screw you!" I lodged another handful of potatoes and gravy at him, and another and another.

A trail of splatters went everywhere, including on Carter's head and another hitting Joe on the temple.

Then something hit my cheek. The piece of roll bounced to the table. My jaw dropped as I stared at Tase, who tossed another chunk at me.

"I had to work," he said. "You of all people should appreciate everything that had to be done to ensure the ski slopes could open."

"I—*of all people*—just want you for once to keep your damn word to me!" More food went flying. "Stop making promises if you have no intention of keeping them!" Two more handfuls. "Because I'm damn sick—" Another chunk— "of the disappointment—" Another— "Of you not being here when you said you'd be, Atanase! Albert! Roca!" A handful punctuated each of his names.

He threw food back, answering each of mine. I could hear both my mother and grandmother gasping and telling us to stop, but my vision was red and all senses focused on the jerk in front of me. Our throws got sloppy, hitting the others, and by the time my frustration was waning, I realized everyone but Saundra was involved.

Then a splat of something hit the side of her head.

Everyone gasped. Her eyes went wide as saucers, her mouth

gaping. Our arms dropped to our sides as we all froze, only our eyes moving as we glanced around. Each of us were covered in potatoes—both white and orange—green bean casserole, stuffing, turkey, cranberry sauce, and gravy. I don't think we even breathed as silence descended, filling the room. Well, besides the sound of food dropping from the chandelier and splatting on the table.

Then Carter burst out laughing. "I got you, Grandma!"

We still held our collective breaths until Saundra finally smiled, a twinkle in her eyes even as she narrowed them. "Yes, you did. But you better watch your back when you're out in the snow later. I prefer snowball fights. A little less messy." She gave me a pointed look before glancing around at the mess. "Clean this up, Adelaide."

She left the room, surely to clean herself up before anyone snatched a picture of one of the coven's High Priestesses and esteemed member of the Court of the Sun and the Moon with a glop of green beans and mashed potatoes clinging to the side of her head.

"We'll help," Joe said, he and Infiniti already grabbing their napkins.

"No worries," Mom said, smiling at me. "We got this."

With a nod, I joined her as we said the spell to right our mess. In no time, Grandmother's pristine dining room was back to normal. She, Joe, and Infiniti began carrying the inedible food back to the kitchen, Joe being appreciative that his mom surely had something for them to eat at his house.

I started to grab the bowl of potatoes when large fingers encircled my wrist. With a tug, I was suddenly sitting on Tase's lap. I refused to look at him, though, my anger still swirling below the surface. Grasping my chin, he turned my head toward him. Food still clung to his closely cut dark hair and eyebrows. I hadn't bothered to magically clean him up.

"I'm really sorry," he murmured, his gray eyes boring into me. "One of the lifts kept getting stuck, and if I didn't get it fixed, opening day would not be happening tomorrow. Then we found a huge tree had fallen, blocking one of the trails, so we had to cut that up."

"Don't you have employees for that?"

"And make them work on Thanksgiving? That was the reason for me going out in the first place, remember?"

I sighed. It had actually been my idea to give his family and other employees the day off.

"And you're so amazing at everything," he continued, "I was sure you had this under control."

I lifted a brow. "Don't you sweet-talk me, mister. You're not off the hook yet."

There was that smirk again. "At least you didn't three-name me this time. That's progress." He leaned his forehead against mine. "I'll make it up to you. I promise. For now, though, let's go crash Michaela and Xandru's dinner."

We didn't quite crash it. Grandmother had already called to see if they had enough food. Some of the inn's guests had to leave unexpectedly, so Michaela said there was plenty. Although there was a lot of bad blood between the Rocas and the Beaumonts—hell, between the Rocas and pretty much everyone, but especially every Old Family—it turned out to be a nice evening.

Later, after Carter had fallen asleep in one of the guest rooms, Tase took my hand and led me outside for a walk. Town square was already lit up with Christmas lights, twinkling as flakes fells around us. We ended up at the ski resort.

"I think you deserve the first runs of the season," Tase said, gesturing at my skis and gear already there, waiting for me.

"Really?" I turned to him, letting him pull me up against him.

"Really. I love you, Bean, and even if you won't be my wife yet, on this day of giving thanks, I'm most grateful to have you in my life." He leaned down and pressed his lips to mine.

After letting the kiss deepen until my heart finally gave in, I pulled away and tilted my head. "Yeah, I guess I'm grateful for you, too, even if you are a bastard."

His brow furrowed. "I thought I was an asshole. Asshole Extraordinaire—I take that title seriously, you know."

Grinning, I leaned up on my toes and gave him another kiss. "Trust me. You can be both. And you're very good at it."

He was also good at showing up even when I'd lost all hope. Maybe I needed to give him a break and say yes. Maybe I had to admit that his love for me was real and lasting.

Maybe . . .

If you haven't already, read Addie and Tase's story starting with *Break Me Not* by Kristie Cook.

SPIRIT OF THE SOLSTICE

BY SEVEN JANE

A Maris & Noelani Short Story

"Okay, take a sip and tell me what you think—and be nice, it's a first attempt."

Fixing her bottom lip firmly between her teeth in anticipation, Maris thrust the martini glass full of creamy red liquid in Simon's direction. The cocktail inside sloshed up the edges. It looked a little too pale for Maris's preference, more blushing pink than holiday red. Maybe she hadn't added enough grenadine to make the color pop? It was her first Christmas cocktail, after all, and her gift for Noelani. It needed to be bright and festive, not dull and boring.

Maris wanted the cocktail redder, like a proper Christmas candy—something that said joy and good tidings, not watered-down holiday cheer.

"No, wait." She retracted her arm before Simon could get his fingers around the stem of the glass, almost spilling it over the flared edge. She added just a couple more drips of the sweet syrup, swirled the liquid to absorb the color, and hooked a candy cane from the glass's rim. After briefly considering the overall effect of the changes and finding it satisfactory—maybe she'd melt some chocolate and add crushed peppermints to the rim on her next attempt?—Maris returned the glass to Simon. "Okay, *now* taste it."

"Are you sure?" he asked, his tone playful. His iridescent eyes shimmered with amusement over the top of the glass, and Maris could tell he was holding back a laugh—presumably at her expense, as usual.

"I'm sure," she confirmed, after only a half second of hesitation. "Yes, sure."

"Are you *sure* you're sure?" Simon pressed, crinkles forming around his eyes.

Maris groaned with exasperation. "Taste it already, Simon!"

The dragon shifter might have been Maris's closest, and certainly most reptilian, friend in Havenwood Falls, but that didn't mean Simon cut her any slack when she got overly imaginative with her bartending. If anything, it made him tease her more each time she concocted a new alcoholic beverage from behind the bar at Fallview Tavern & Grill, where they worked—which was basically an everyday occurrence, seeing as how many of the town's drinkers liked to get creative.

The town's supernatural inhabitants and humans alike had a particular fondness for flavored vodkas, and Maris had experimented with everything from zucchini manhattans to blueberry white Russians. Still, even though he teased her, Simon was always a willing taste-tester for Maris's creations, and he was always kind with his criticism when he offered it. He also interceded on her behalf with Odette Alverson, the tavern's proprietress, who didn't love how quickly Maris poured through the bar's stock. There was a tension between Maris and Odette that Maris didn't think could be attributed purely to her work behind the bar, though. She thought it might have something to do with her girlfriend, Noelani, the naiad who had spent the past few decades cursed after an incident with Maris's father over twenty years before—a terrible tragedy that even Maris hadn't known about until she'd been called by the town's magic to Havenwood Falls.

Maris had broken Noelani's curse and with it the spell of dark cold that had surrounded her well deep in the forest of Havenwood Falls, but Odette's icy hospitality toward Maris had only thawed to barely lukewarm. Both Noelani and Simon had assured her that Odette's chilly reception wasn't personal and that not all creatures in Havenwood Falls were meant to be friendly toward one another, but Maris nonetheless kept trying to win the woman over.

So far, it didn't look likely.

But that was a problem for another day. Today, Maris just had to get her newest cocktail perfect. It was December 21st, the winter solstice, and tonight she and Noelani would be celebrating their first holiday together. Buying for a naiad was next to impossible, so a crafty cocktail was the best, most personalized gift Maris could think of. She closed her eyes and squeezed her hands together as, with a final, lingering exhale, Simon raised the glass to his lips and inhaled the sweet aroma of her newest concoction.

With her eyes closed, Maris heard Simon sniff again, and she couldn't take the anticipation any longer. Peeking out from one eye to see him eyeing the beverage suspiciously, Maris groaned again.

"Seriously, I'm two seconds from pouring it down your throat," she growled. "Taste it already." It probably wasn't wise to threaten a dragon, but, oh well.

"What's in it?" Simon asked, suspicion coloring the edges of his words. He laughed good-naturedly when Maris sighed in exasperation. "You'll forgive me if I ask. You've been known to put weird things in cocktails, and I don't trust anything this red without asking first—not in a place like Havenwood Falls."

"You *literally* just watched me add in more grenadine," Maris moaned. Simon shrugged apologetically. "Fine," she caved. "It's mostly white chocolate liqueur, vodka, peppermint schnapps, a tiny bit of half and half, and the *grenadine*"—she emphasized this last—"and that's a candy cane hanging from the edge, just in case you weren't sure. Now, drink! We've got to get back to the well before sunset, and it's already noon. Daylight is ticking, Simon." She snapped her fingers impatiently.

Whether satisfied with her explanation or propelled by her sense of urgency, Simon took a small sip.

"Well?" Maris pressed once he'd swallowed.

The dragon shifter licked his lips.

"It's surprisingly delicious," he decided, and Maris felt every muscle in her body unclench.

"Surprisingly?" she asked, retrieving the glass to take a sip for herself. It *was* delicious—just the right creaminess, and just the right amount of mint, too. "When do I ever make something not delicious?"

Simon finally let go of the laugh he'd been holding. "Remember when you thought it would be fun to make a 'fruit salad martini'?"

Maris remembered, though she certainly preferred not to.

"What are you calling this one?" Simon asked.

"This," Maris pointed at the bright red cocktail, which had already been deemed a success, "is my version of a peppermintini. Mint, cream, and just a touch of holiday spirit—get it? Now that I've got the measurements perfect, I'm going to mix a big batch of it for our celebration tonight. You're still coming, right?"

Noelani had insisted that Simon join them for their solstice gathering, saying something about having an odd number of guests was unlucky. By Maris's count, adding Simon made three, which by her math *was* an odd number, but her girlfriend had claimed that including Simon made four. And, since Noelani often had her own way of doing things, Maris had let it go. She was glad to have Simon join them, and if inviting him somehow made an even four, then so be it.

"Wouldn't miss it," Simon said. He helped Maris gather the necessary equipment for mixing and bottling her newest cocktail.

It took most of the remaining daylight to pack up the jug of Maris's peppermintini, and when they were done, Maris and Simon piled into Simon's truck.

"To the well?" he asked when they had finally warmed up enough to talk. A fresh dusting of snow was coming down, adding another layer of white to the already snow-covered town. Maris was glad she'd taken up Simon's advice and stocked up on winter gear, because otherwise she'd have frozen solid weeks ago.

"One quick stop first. I promised Noelani we'd swing by Howe's

Herbal Shoppe on our way. She special ordered something, and we need to pick it up."

"A special order from Howe's Herbal?" Simon quirked an eyebrow. "That sounds interesting."

"Life is always interesting with Noelani." Maris laughed. It was true—and one of the things Maris loved most about her sweet naiad. Usually, Maris had a hard time sitting still for too long, growing easily bored with whatever was going on around her. Because of her restlessness, Maris had spent her life hopscotching around the globe, remaining rootless and free. It was less a lifestyle and more a survival mechanism, since Maris had worried she'd get stuck if she stayed anywhere too long. She'd already been in Havenwood Falls for eight months, but so far, Maris hadn't had the slightest opportunity to grow bored. Between all the curiosities of the town and the growing attachment she felt to Noelani every day, Maris was becoming more and more hopeful she'd never leave the box canyon. There was still so much left here to discover, including coming to terms with her own family's past, which she had yet to do. Her father had left a stain on their family name in Havenwood Falls, and Maris intended to clear it, whether she stayed in town or not. She just hoped it would be enough to still her gypsy heart.

When they arrived at Howe's Herbal, Rose Howe was waiting for them.

"Hi, Rose," Maris greeted her. "I'm here to pick up Noelani's order."

"You're just in time. We just finished it," Rose said. She turned and walked to a small room where additional inventory was kept, and Maris gazed at her as she left. Like Noelani, Rose had beautiful long red hair. Sometimes when she saw Rose around town, Maris would think she'd seen Noelani, and her heart would skip a beat until she realized it wasn't her. Noelani rarely left her meadow in the forest. Now that her curse was broken, people had begun to visit her well again, and she wanted to be there if they came, though she and Maris had agreed that she'd wear sunglasses now, just in case any new dangers found their way to her. Some of Noelani's magic was passed through her glimpses, and after the curse that had consumed her well when Noelani's eyes had met those of Peter Heilen, Maris's father, the naiad was hesitant to let her gaze wander freely among strangers.

In time, Maris hoped that Noelani would venture farther into Havenwood Falls, but she hadn't pressured her. Noelani, the Lady of the Water, would leave her well and come to town when she was ready. There was no reason to rush her, especially when Maris was still so unsure what their future held.

"Here it is," Rose announced upon her return, her voice weighed down under the strain of a large, cylindrical shaped package the height of a small person. She delivered it with an *oof* into Simon's arms. Luckily, being a shifter, the guy had a lot of surplus strength, and so he held the package easily, although even he seemed surprised at its heft.

"What on earth is that?" Maris asked.

It took Rose a second to collect her breath.

"A candle, actually," she said, pushing the words out between lungfuls of air.

"A big one," added Simon.

"No kidding," Maris returned, still eyeing the shape. She fished for her wallet. "What do we owe you?"

"No charge. It's a trade." Rose waved away Maris's credit card. "The wax Noelani will send back more than compensates for the time pouring it."

Maris blinked and slung her purse strap back over her shoulder, accepting the mystery as a good enough answer. Threes that equal four, trading candle wax the size of a small child…as odd as it was, things like this just made sense in Havenwood Falls.

"Happy holidays, Rose. Give my love to Scarlet as well." Maris waved goodbye to Rose as she helped Simon maneuver the gigantic candle out of the small shop.

"Please tell me there's no other stops?" Simon asked when they were safely back in the truck. Between the large container of Maris's peppermintini, the huge candle, and all the other assorted odds and ends stuffed into the cab with them, they were quickly running out of room.

"No more stops," Maris confirmed. "Although you've got to carry that bad boy all the way through the forest."

"Good thing I'm strong." Simon laughed. "That thing is almost as tall as you, like it's a whole other person. Now we know who Guest Number Four is."

Maris laughed in agreement as they made their way to the edge of the forest that encircled Noelani's well, still wishing she knew exactly what her girlfriend was up to.

They arrived in the clearing to find Noelani hard at work above ground.

She had, incredibly, managed to haul a huge log out of the forest that was easily three times as big as the candle. It looked more like a fallen tree trunk than a log, and how she'd gotten it all the way into the clearing was just another one of the magical mysteries Maris could catalog with the rest that she'd acquired in her time in Havenwood Falls.

Noelani had decorated the log-slash-tree trunk with all sorts of beautiful items she'd collected from the meadow, as well as some of the flowers and trinkets those that visited her well had left her. Bright red holly berries and evergreens were scattered upon it, woven through with strands of hair and ribbon, and she was currently busy surrounding its base with a border of carefully placed pinecones and acorns that dotted the snow. Several plates of steaming food were set along the well's stone brim, and four chairs had been set in an intentional semi-circle around the log.

"What's this?" Maris asked, setting down the items she'd carried to embrace Noelani. She pointed to the log.

"A Yule log, of course." Noelani laughed and hugged her back. She brushed a quick kiss against Maris's lips before nodding approvingly at the candle Simon was busy unwrapping, then returned to add the finishing touches on her log.

Maris had heard of a Yule log, but she'd never seen one.

"It's beautiful," she said, watching as Noelani bustled about, using the paper wrapping Simon had discarded from the candle to form a pile of kindling. "I'd expected a Christmas tree."

"We could decorate a tree," Noelani mused, "but the Yule log is a much older tradition, and I thought it would be more appropriate for tonight's solstice celebration."

Maris glanced at Simon, who shrugged, then turned back to Noelani.

"Isn't it the same thing?" she asked, hoping the question wouldn't be offensive. Noelani might look like a young woman, but neither she nor Maris had any idea exactly how old she actually was. Naiads lived a very, very long time, and in the scheme of Noelani's lifespan, Christmas was a relatively new tradition.

"Not exactly, but similar," Noelani continued on, and if she was put off by the question, she didn't show it. "The Yule log is a relic of ancient pagan celebrations around this time of year that honored the dark and celebrated the return of the light. Once the sun sets on the solstice, the longest night of the year, they'd do exactly what we are going to do tonight: set the Yule log ablaze in a clearing, and feast, sing, and dance around it until morning as we await the symbolic return of the sun, and with it, the lengthening of days that will lead us back to spring. The idea is that if we keep the log burning, its light will call back the sun."

However unfamiliar to the traditions that Maris had always celebrated, Noelani's idea of a solstice celebration sounded like one hell of a party—and if there was something Maris could get behind, it was a party.

"Feast and sing and dance…and drink?" she asked hopefully.

Noelani laughed and moved back to Maris, pulling her into her arms. "And drink," she confirmed. "What kind of celebration would it be without drink?"

Maris was too busy staring into Noelani's eyes to answer. The woman was so beautiful, and so precious to her.

"Good then, because we came prepared," Simon said from outside their little love bubble. He lifted up the jug of peppermintini. "Maris has outdone even herself."

"Is that so?" Noelani teased. She released Maris and slid alongside Simon, eyeing the red fluid that sloshed from behind the large glass container. "One of your special potions?"

It was Maris's turn to laugh. "Something like that, although my magic might be a little more of the alcoholic variety than the actually magical." She giggled. "It's my newest recipe—a peppermintini, the perfect holiday cocktail." She blushed. "It was the only thing I could think of to give you...the only thing that really felt like it came from me, and not from a store."

"It sounds divine," said Noelani, and Maris could tell she meant it.

"It is," Simon confirmed.

"Then I think we've got everything," Noelani said, listing off items, which she counted on her fingertips. "The log, the fire starter"—she pointed at Simon, who rolled his eyes in mock protest—"the drink, and the candle. Now all we need is our Christmas star." She stooped and wrapped her arms around the candle that stood nearly to her waist, and inhaled deeply.

"Okay, I give," Maris chimed in. "The Yule log, I get. What's the purpose of the candle?"

Noelani rested her hand tenderly atop the candle, testing the strength of the wick between her fingertips. "Well, it's served many over the years, and it changes from place to place. Like the fire in the Yule log, the candle must burn throughout the night, but while we celebrate around the log, the candle is a bit more...shall we say, invitational?"

"Invitational?" both Simon and Maris echoed.

"Are we expecting company?" asked Maris afterward. "Simon and I kind of assumed the person-sized candle was our fourth guest."

Noelani laughed. "Not exactly," she said, "but you could interpret it that way. This year, we have not one special guest, but two. It's very bad luck to have an odd number of people in attendance for our solstice meal."

This time, Maris was too curious to be satisfied with a magical riddle. "But how would *you* interpret it, my love?" she coaxed, hoping Noelani would elaborate. Simon must have agreed, as he joined Maris where she had decided to sit around the soon-to-be-lit Yule log. "You, me, and Simon make three—who is our fourth guest? And what's this about a Christmas star—I thought we were celebrating solstice?"

"I'll tell you everything around the fire," Noelani volunteered as she handed Simon a piece of kindling. The sun had just slid fully behind the curtain of snow-covered pine, and twilight was upon them. "If Simon will be so kind."

Accepting the bundle of wadded up paper and dried pine needles, Simon turned his back for privacy and let out a deep breath. When he twisted back around, the kindling was a big ball of fire. Having a dragon around was a lot more handy than fussing with matches.

Noelani accepted the fire and touched it to both ends of the log, then the wick of the candle. When all was blazing brightly, she sat down across from Maris and Simon. "The winter solstice is about more than the seasonal change from dark back to light. It's the perfect time to receive visitors and prepare for a new season of light and magic. The Yule log is part of that ritual, as is the candle, though it serves another purpose—it not only acts as a guiding light, but as a sort of conductor for magic."

"Is that why Rose wants the wax back?" Maris asked, remembering what Rose had said when they'd collected the candle.

"Precisely," confirmed Noelani. "Once the candle burns out, some of the wax will go into my well to imbue my waters. Some will be given to the witches and herbalists in town to aid in their spell casting and potions-making, and the rest will be planted around Havenwood Falls, to protect our home. The wax of the Yule candle is as much a gift after it's been burned as it is while it burns."

"And while it burns has something to do with our surprise visitor?" Maris asked, trying to get back to her original question. "Which, I'm guessing, has something to do with a star?"

Noelani nodded, and Maris could tell she was hunting for the right words to respond in a way that would answer all of Maris's questions at once. "It does. You see, winter is a season of death and rebirth. The solstice is the darkest night of the year, and it's just as important to honor the return of the sun that will bring literal light back to our lives as it is to remember those who are no longer with us, for they share the dark and their memory can likewise shine through the more spiritual darkness of the end of the year."

Maris considered this, and she didn't like that word *spiritual*. "Those that are no longer with us... Are you talking about ghosts, like...Christmas Ghosts? Ebenezer Scrooge, style? I haven't been that grumpy this season, have I?"

She laughed nervously, trying not to sound as uncomfortable as she suddenly felt.

Simon snorted beside her, and she elbowed him for it.

"Of course not," Noelani laughed. She didn't say anything about the ghosts, though.

"But I thought Halloween was for ghosts," Maris argued. "That's the night the dead come back to haunt the living and all that. I never thought about Christmas—or the solstice, I guess—as a time for ghost stories."

"Oh, but there have been ghosts at Christmas, and stories about them," interjected Simon. "In fact, some of the best Christmas tales are about ghosts."

Maris shivered, and the chill that fell over her had nothing to do with the cold. After the events of the past summer, she'd made a point of avoiding this years' Halloween and Samhain goings-on in Havenwood Falls. Likewise, Maris hadn't forgotten the horrific form that had taken possession of Noelani before she'd found her, or the terrifying creatures that had permeated the forest surrounding Noelani's well during the curse. She did not relish the idea of meeting them again.

"Sorry," she said, trying not to sound like a downer. "But I'll be honest—that's two more ghost visits per year than I'm entirely comfortable with right now."

Noelani reached across to squeeze Maris's knee reassuringly, and Simon hugged her in the crook of his arm.

"We are all surrounded by ghosts all year," Noelani said. "Some good, some bad…and some more than others. But this isn't a haunting, or anything to fear. It's a different sort of visit—a living memory, if you will. The winter solstice is a time to remember family, and tonight, the darkest night of the year, is the night that we receive visitors—the family members and loved ones who have left us—back into our homes so that we can celebrate the coming of light and the new year together. Think of it more like a memory, than a ghost."

Family. The word sounded like an alarm in Maris's thoughts. There was only one family member she could think of, and he was not someone she wanted to see—nor would be welcome, dead or alive, in Havenwood Falls.

"You don't…" Maris swallowed a ball that had risen into her throat back down into her stomach. "You don't mean my father, do you?"

Noelani clapped her hands over her mouth and, for a moment, appeared genuinely horrified. "No, of course not!" she exclaimed. "I think we're all agreed *he* is not invited. But there is someone else I think you deserve to meet, Maris. Someone who might help you—help all of us—move past that dreadful day. Receiving her on our solstice celebration is, I think, the best gift I could give you."

Maris barely had time to digest what Noelani said when the first drip of wax slid down the side of the great pillar candle. The burning wood crackled meaningfully, and something shifted in the air around them. Maris watched in awe as the candle's flame flickered, growing larger, and an image began to form inside its light.

The image grew larger and more defined, taking on the shape of a woman made of fire and light. When at last the figure was fully formed, it stepped out of the flame and into the fire-lit, snowy night of the winter solstice, and became as solid as Simon's arm around her and Noelani's palm on her knee. A woman—their fourth visitor—joined them in their circle around the flickering Yule log.

Maris gasped, and the sudden spring of tears momentarily clouded her vision as she took in the woman standing before her. She appeared near in age to Maris's own, with lovely tawny skin, large doe-like eyes that were the sort that spent their time gazing at the stars, and long, gingerbread curls that fell in rolling tumbles down her back. Maris recognized the woman instantly from the single photograph she'd seen of her—the one she'd looked at over and over again since she'd first heard the tale of the woman in the picture, each time wondering if she was doomed to suffer the same, loveless fate as her father.

The drowning bride.

"Stella," Maris named the woman, and Stella smiled in return.

"You have your father's eyes," Stella said, touching her ghostly fingertips atop Maris's chest. "But not his heart."

The first tear fell down Maris's cheek as Stella settled herself on the seat beside Noelani, then another, and another. She watched as the two women embraced, all the while trying to find the right words to apologize for a crime she hadn't committed, but one that had been her affliction to bear—even when she hadn't known she'd bore it. Maris's father was the reason that Stella was a ghost and not a living, breathing woman who could enjoy the holiday with her own family and not as the spectral visitor of a nighttime forest. And even though Maris had had no part in his evil, she still felt accountable for it, as if his darkness has passed onto it.

She hadn't known it at the time, but she thought now that darkness was the thing she'd been running from this whole time—the thing she'd been trying to leave behind her every time she pulled out of another job, another city. She'd feared that the monster that had claimed her father's heart might have hold on hers, too, and so she'd lived her life as her father had—always running from love, from commitment, from anything that would take up room in her heart that belonged to something eager to consume it as its own. All of that running had led Maris back to Noelani, but even now she had kept one foot in and one foot out of Havenwood Falls, regardless of how badly she wanted to call this place home.

"I'm so sorry," Maris blurted out to Stella. "I'm so sorry for what my father did to you."

Stella's face was impassive, darkening for just a brief moment before her features lit up into a smile so bright that Maris thought it might outshine the flickering log in front of them. She reached out and clasped Maris's hand in hers.

"I forgive him," Stella said. "And I forgive you for whatever burden you hold as your own. I am free now, and so you are, Maris. Your father cannot hurt either one of us any longer, and whatever evil that lived with him is gone with him."

"Thank you," was all that Maris could say.

Standing beside her, Simon wiped his face and pretended the smoke of the fire was making his eyes water. "A toast then?" he suggested, uncorking the jug of Maris's peppermintini and filling four cups to the top. He pulled a handful of candy canes from his coat pocket and hooked their bends, just as Maris had done, to the glass rims, then offered one to Noelani, to Maris, and to Stella. "To new beginnings," he said, "and to family and friends."

He raised his glass, and the three women joined him.

"To love," said Noelani.

"To light," said Maris.

"And to happily ever afters," Stella added, and when the four of them had finished their toast, Stella took Noelani's hand in one of hers and Maris's in the other, and began to sing.

Read Maris and Noelani's story in *Of Salt and Stars* by Seven Jane and Stella's story in *The Drowning Bride* also by Seven Jane.

A MISTLETOE WEDDING

BY SUSAN BURDORF

A Rusty & Sherry Short Story

*H*avenwood Falls looked positively magical with all the lights and decorations of the holiday season around town. Shop windows displayed toys that captivated children and adults, alike. Festive garlands were strung, some lighted and some smelling of fresh pine from the surrounding woods.

The town really shows up for the season every year, thought Sherry, smiling in satisfaction as if she had anything to do with the decorating. Of course, with the skiing and general quaint air of the town, the decorations were more for the tourists and the human residents than the rest of the town. As a human, living with and loving a supernatural resident, Sherry saw everything from both sides, and she was okay with that.

Sherry breathed in all her favorite scents of the season as shop doors opened and closed around her. Conversations floated past her as did the folks buying the amazing offerings from the shops. She saw a lot of the distinctive colored bags from the herb shop of her dear friend Ruby Howe and her family, and the white bags with gold music notes meant some had been to Cece's music shop as well. All over the place were happy, smiling faces as purchasers compared their items and oohed and aahed over what they'd bought.

She stepped inside Coffee Haven and stopped for a second to let her eyes adjust to the interior. The snow that coated the sidewalks and town outside was just bright enough to make the difference like night and day when walking inside the adorably decorated coffee shop, her favorite place to spend the day when she had a writing project with a deadline to meet.

The cabin she and Rusty shared up the mountain was great for alone time as well, especially when it was just the two of them. She smiled at the memory of their lovemaking last night then shook herself back to the present. She had things to do, and dwelling on Rusty was *not* going to get those pages written—although he was great inspiration for the scene she was set to write today.

She waved to Harlow and Willow, who waved back before helping their next customer. Looking around the crowded room, she tried to find a spot she could occupy for the next few hours.

She noticed her favorite table had just been vacated and made a beeline for it. The table semi-faced the street so she could people watch if she wanted to, but was also tucked into a corner where it got the least amount of inside traffic in the busy shop. But what really attracted her to that location was the nearby electric outlet. She expected to work her computer pretty hard today, and having to recharge it too often wouldn't be fun at all. She hated being stopped in the middle of a great scene, which a dead battery would certainly do.

She could smell the strong odors of peppermint, cinnamon, lavender, and of course, coffee. She grinned as a steaming cup of said beverage was set in front of her by one of the baristas at Coffee Haven. They didn't normally bring the coffee to the customers, but she and Harlow had a special arrangement. Harlow knew exactly what she liked and how she liked it.

"Thank you, Harlow," Sherry said with joy lighting her face. Coffee was the nectar of the Gods, and she didn't care what Rusty said about it being an obsession with her. She would die happy if she had a cup of this magic brew in her hands. "I so need this right now."

Harlow chuckled. "I'll be by in a little bit to see if you need more."

Sherry took a quick sip of the magic brew and nodded. Pulling out her laptop, she plugged it in and began reading her current novel. Within minutes, she was lost in the world of Heartwood Glen, the magical kingdom of her story.

Writing this novel was therapeutic for Sherry, who'd arrived in Havenwood Falls after a disastrous break-up from her fiancé and found Rusty almost immediately. Their love story was the basis for the first book. She was now currently working on the second novel in the series while the first one was making the rounds of agents and publishers. So far the novel had been rejected a few times, but she had hopes the story of a paranormal town with human and supernatural residents would strike a chord with an agent and be selected for publication.

So intent was she on the story, she didn't hear when Harlow returned with a second coffee. But she smelled it. Taking a break, she sipped and smiled at the young woman, who glanced at the screen and chuckled.

"How are you doing, Susan . . . haha . . . I mean, Sherry?" said Harlow. Her comment was followed by a dramatic wink and mischievous grin.

Sherry grinned back at Harlow's reference to her alias. She'd decided to write the story with a pen name to protect the town she'd come to love. Plus, it made her feel freer to write the true story of her love for Rusty by using a name other than her own.

Leaning forward so no one else could hear her, Harlow said, "I beta-read those chapters you sent me and, girrrl . . . steamy!" She pretended to fan herself. "Writing under a pen name is smart. Where'd you come up with the name Susan Burdorf, anyway?"

Sherry blushed. "I'm glad you liked those chapters. I am working on the last scene right now. Should be better than the others. I hope so, anyway. I heard the name somewhere and just liked it."

Before Harlow moved off to clear a nearby table, she said, "You will let me read them, right?"

"Of course," Sherry said as she turned back to her laptop. "I better get back to work. Keep the coffee coming," she said as Harlow walked away.

"You bet!" Harlow called back over her shoulder.

Several hours later, four empty coffee containers and a lot of crumbs from blueberry scones littered the table around her. Sherry straightened her neck and looked outside. The town was darkening, twinkling lights adding to the fairytale effect of the town square. She loved Havenwood Falls at the holidays.

Harlow and Willow, Coffee Haven's owner, were chatting with customers and clearing tables. The noise inside Coffee Haven was a steady flow of laughter and conversation. Sherry decided to take a last look at her email before leaving. She was shocked to see it was almost five o'clock. She'd been here for nearly six hours!

"Another cup?" Harlow asked as she swung by on her way to clear another table.

"Uh-huh," Sherry said, barely registering Harlow's question.

"Everything okay? You look a little—" Harlow began.

"A little shocked?" Sherry finished for her. Her face was flushed. She couldn't believe what she was reading.

She scanned the email quickly, then read it again.

"Really, Sherry, you're scaring me a bit. What's in that email?"

"Nothing much . . . just something that might change my life. Forever." Sherry said the last word in a whisper.

She read the email again. And then again.

"I would love to meet with you to discuss this amazing story you sent me based off the pitch contest you entered. Please contact me at the above phone number as soon as you can.

~ Stacey Grahamson, agent Oliphant Agency"

Sherry physically reached up and closed her mouth. For real. An agent wanted to talk about her story. An agent wanted her to call her about her story. Sherry couldn't believe it.

She scanned the email for the agent's phone number and dialed with shaking fingers. She wasn't even sure she'd dialed it correctly until she heard the woman's voice on the other end of the line.

"Hello." The woman sounded hesitant, and Sherry was sure she didn't recognize the number. To be honest, Sherry was surprised she answered and didn't want Sherry to leave a voicemail.

"Hello. This is Sherry Grimes. I received an email from you. At least, I think it was you. Are you, Stacey Grahamson?"

"Yes, I am." The woman on the line sounded suddenly sure of herself. "And you are the author of Heartwood Glen, right?"

"Yes," Sherry said, her voice sounding squeaky even to her own ears.

"I'm so glad you called me."

"I'm so glad you answered my call," Sherry said. Truthfully, she wasn't sure what else to say and was grateful when the other woman took over the conversation.

"Is this a good time to talk?" she started, and Sherry agreed it was a great time to talk.

"Good. I have your story pulled up right now on my laptop, and I have to tell you, I loved reading it. As a matter of fact, I loved it so much I had to email you right away to see if you were interested in having me represent you and this story. I think we can do great things with this. I see movies or maybe a TV series in its future. You mentioned you are working on a sequel?"

"Yes," Sherry said. "I'm working on it now. It's called Return to Heartwood Glen and is about—"

"If it's all the same to you, let's spend this call talking about your recent submission. I definitely want to hear about the second book, but I have some questions and suggestions about the first book. Do you have a little time to talk now?"

Sherry glanced out the window at the growing evening and thought about Rusty coming home to an empty cabin. Her hesitation caught the attention of Stacey, who breathed deeply down the line.

"Tell you what. I am looking at the clock and realize it is seven o'clock here. What time is it by you?"

"Five o'clock. We're two hours behind you." Sherry did the math quickly in her head.

"Okay, how about if we talk tomorrow? I know it's Christmas Eve, but I'd love to get started before we close down for the holidays. Say ten o'clock your time? That's noon for me."

"Yes, that's great."

"I'll send you a contract by email, if that's okay? I want to have you look it over in case you might have questions about how this works. Oh, you aren't represented yet, are you?"

"N-n-no, I'm not," Sherry said. She hung up the call a few minutes later and couldn't move.

"Sherry, you okay?" Harlow touched her on the shoulder, and Sherry jumped.

"Um . . . yes, yes, I'm fine." Sherry knew she was grinning like the proverbial Cheshire Cat, but she couldn't stop.

"Hey, there's Rusty." Harlow pointed out the window, and Sherry looked up in time to see it was indeed Rusty slipping a small bag inside his jacket before hurrying through the snow to his truck that was parked nearby. She wasn't sure how she'd missed the truck. It was pretty distinctive.

"I better get going. He'll be wondering where I am."

Sherry grabbed her laptop and put everything in her bag. "Thanks for everything today, Harlow. I appreciate the coffees."

"Anytime," Harlow shouted as Sherry walked out the door. "Gotta keep one of our favorite customers happy."

Sherry waved over her shoulder as she slipped between a few customers walking in as she walked out.

Later, when she and Rusty were snuggled up on the couch, Sherry sighed in contentment.

Rusty pulled her into a tighter embrace, and she breathed in the outdoors that was always part of his scent, as well as the strong odor of the wolf that was also part of who he was. As a matter of fact, the wolf was what she had met first and was the part of him she loved more than anything else.

There had never been anyone else for her once she'd met Rusty, and he constantly reminded her of that fact whenever she was hesitant to admit her feelings for him were as strong as his for her. She was his soul mate, the only one he could ever be totally free with, and that knowledge made her love him more deeply than she'd ever believed was possible.

The time before Havenwood Falls was a blur. Her life back then held no pull for her. Rusty was her world, and their life here in Havenwood Falls was her now and forever. Melodramatic as it was, she couldn't imagine a reason for ever leaving here. Yet, the call with the agent had stirred something in her that she wasn't prepared for. She wanted to sell her story, she wanted to be an author, and this might be the first step in realizing her dream. Why, then, was she holding back from telling Rusty about it?

Sherry closed her eyes, slowed her breathing, tried to calm herself down, but somehow all her attempts were merely making her more wound up. Tomorrow's phone call could change her whole world in ways she never imagined . . . or nothing might happen at all. She hadn't opened up her email yet. She and Rusty had an unwritten rule that before he took his wolf form and left for the night rounds in the woods, which he was responsible for as the sheriff department's forest ranger, they would spend time together. Usually this was her favorite part of the day, but tonight she wanted him to leave. Selfish of her, she knew, but Sherry was a bundle of nerves waiting for his departure.

Rusty, as if sensing her pensive mood, kissed the top of her head and sighed, sounding more like a soft growl deep in his chest, signaling a little of his wolf was beginning to show itself. Not that Sherry ever minded that beast's appearance. "I have to go in a few minutes. But I feel like you're not like yourself tonight. Are you okay? Anything you need to tell me?"

Curses, she thought. *How does he always know me so well?*

Instead of answering, she shook her head, careful to keep her expression neutral.

"Just tired, I guess. I've been working quite a bit on the story." She bit her lip. She hadn't meant to bring up the story. She hoped her tone hadn't given her away. His reaction proved he was as distracted as she was, as his usual Sherry-radar didn't seem to be on full tilt tonight.

Instead of pursuing her mood, he pulled her to him, settling her on his lap so they faced each other. Slipping her arms around his neck, Sherry smiled, pulling her emotions together. Shaking her head, she shrugged and said, "You know how nervous I get when you have to go on patrol. I'm just a little anxious about you being out there. The weather can change so quickly here, especially in winter."

Rusty frowned. He pulled her into an embrace, nuzzling her neck in a way that never failed to cause a rise in the temperature of their body heat. She squirmed into a more comfortable position, her body tight against his, breasts pressing into his chest, the smell of him sending her heart into overdrive.

"I have time," he whispered into her neck as he continued his slow progression of kisses from the hollow of her throat to the collarbone and along her chest until he reached the swell of her breasts. He buried his face in between her breasts and gently moved her lacy bra down the swells to reveal her nipples, which he teased with his tongue.

She moaned, whispering in a tight passion-flamed growl that rivaled his earlier one. "What are we wasting time for?"

He laughed, a deep-throated chuckle that sent chills of anticipation down her spine. Picking her up, he continued kissing her as they made their way to the bedroom, his arms cradling her as he laid her on the bed, not missing a kiss.

She answered his rising need with her own, arching her back to make release of her jeans from her body easier. She unbuttoned his shirt, slipping it from his shoulders with a slow strip-tease that had him breathless with desire, signaled by his shrug of shoulders to fling his shirt to the floor. Intimate clothing followed outer clothes to land in disarray around the room. Furs on the bed were pulled on top of the couple as they found purchase and began a slow and familiar dance of love that never ceased to arouse them both.

Gasping, they climaxed together then rocked their bodies up to a second level of ecstasy before collapsing against each other, sated and sweaty. Sherry licked the sweat from Rusty's shoulder, nipping him slightly.

"I have to leave . . ."

"I know," Sherry said continuing to nip his shoulder then collarbone then throat as he'd done to start their lovemaking. He pulled her face to him and kissed her with such pure love that Sherry felt the heat rising in her again. Her eyes widened in surprise at the ferocity with which he kissed her, as if he was trying to stake his claim again, even knowing he'd already won her.

"I love you, Sherry," he whispered when he pulled his mouth from hers.

Sherry traced the contours of his cheeks, rubbing the tips of her fingers along his jaw, loving the feel of his unshaven face in her hands. His beauty never ceased to surprise and excite her. She still couldn't believe her luck in finding this man, and the fact that he was a wolf shifter and she a human never bothered her.

She would take and love every moment with her immortal man. Even knowing they couldn't have forever, she would take these moments and bottle them away in her memory. Theirs was a love that transcended time, and she had learned in the last few years with him that loving someone so completely would never be wrong.

She kissed his hands, loving each finger that brought such pleasure to her body and heart then sat up, pulling one of the furs around her.

Glancing at the clock next to the bed, she sighed and fell back against the pillows.

He kissed the tip of her nose and rose from the bed. Sherry watched his lithe body move across the room with a grace that always made her heart skip a beat. He was beautiful and her perfect match. They were content as things were. Havenwood Falls didn't hold with convention when it came to mating, and their living together wasn't a sin here. She wasn't too worried about what anyone thought anyway. She and her former boyfriend, Brad—a human she'd been engaged to before finding out he was cheating on her then running away to Havenwood Falls and into the arms of Rusty Higgins in full wolf form

—had been living together too. But Brad had nothing on Rusty when it came to loyalty and love.

Rusty won all comparisons, hands down.

But Rusty was practically immortal. And more and more, Sherry thought about that—about how much time they had. She looked up at the ceiling. How could she regret their love and life together? How could she doubt this was where she belonged?

Perhaps it was wishing for a permanence that brought her to this confusion.

Rusty came back into view fully dressed now for his nighttime patrol in jeans and flannel shirt, rubbing his damp hair.

Once he reached the woods, he would shed the clothes and begin his patrols that would keep him out all night. She sat up, crooked her finger, and smiled at him in her best coquettish manner. He grinned like a schoolboy meeting his crush under the bleachers on Friday night.

"By the moon, woman, you know I have to go," he said, leaning onto the bed until his lips were seconds away from kissing her.

"Surely you can spare a girl a kiss . . . or two . . . thousand," she whispered. She met his eyes, love shining between them like a tangible thread.

He laughed. Ruffling her hair, he stepped back.

"I will see you soon."

She blew him a kiss and flounced back onto the bed, wrapped in the furs that still smelled of their lovemaking. She waited until she was sure he was gone. Once the silence became familiar, she slipped from bed and padded nude to the bathroom, where she showered and dressed in his discarded flannel shirt, which reached halfway down her thighs and smelled strongly of his male scent.

She made herself a cup of coffee, returning to the living room where she flipped open her laptop. The screen brightened, and she scrolled through her emails until she found the one she was looking for.

She hesitated before opening it. Not sure why she was being so melodramatic.

A half hour later, she was still staring at the screen in disbelief.

Someone wanted her book. Someone thought it was amazing. Someone loved her words.

She wasn't sure her heart could take this realization that her book was in someone else's mind, and not just hers. Yes, Harlow loved it, but Harlow was a friend. This was someone who didn't know her, someone who had never met her before.

Now what?

"Well, you take that leap, that's what," she told herself. Closing her eyes, she pushed the enter button on her return of the contract and said a quick prayer that she'd made the right decision. Heartwood Glen was with an agent. *Wow. Just wow.*

Sherry got up and paced around the room for a few minutes. Her coffee was cold, and she took the mug to the microwave to reheat it then forgot about it and returned to bed where she tossed and turned until dawn, when Rusty returned home.

He slipped into bed, his body warmed by his wolf fur and smelling of pine trees and starlit skies. Sherry snuggled up to him and fell into a deep sleep, all thoughts of her book forgotten in the harbor of her lover's arms.

She left the cabin with Rusty later that morning, heading to Coffee Haven for a quick cup of coffee before meeting her friends Ruby and Cece for some last-minute shopping and their traditional Christmas Eve lunch. Rusty gave her a quick kiss and drove off toward the police station where he was to have a meeting with Sheriff Kasun. They planned to meet up for dinner at Napoli's before heading home. She wasn't even sure they'd be open on Christmas Eve, but with a mysterious grin, Rusty had insisted on meeting her there. And she'd learned a long time ago that what Rusty wanted, he usually got. Not that she minded a bit.

Sherry found Coffee Haven packed with skiers and tourists,

leaving neither Harlow nor Willow time to chat. She grabbed her coffee and wove her way between the throngs on the sidewalks around town until she got to the herb shop where Ruby and Cece were waiting for her.

The three were done shopping and seated for lunch before Sherry had time to think. In no time, their orders were in front of them, and Cece, who as an angel didn't eat much, picked at the salad she'd ordered.

Sherry glanced out the window and saw the town's workers decorating the gazebo in the town square park. It was beginning to look like a fairy tale castle with white tulle drapes secured around the pillars, sparkling white lights, garlands of pine from the forest, and small sprigs of something she assumed was mistletoe hanging in spaces around the gazebo secured with white ribbon.

"How beautiful." Sherry pointed to the gazebo. The other two followed her finger and nodded their approval. "What's going on over there? I've never seen the gazebo decorated that way before."

"Yes. I'm not sure why they decided to decorate the gazebo this year so fancy, but someone requested it. It is quite pretty. Certainly adds something extra magical to the whole atmosphere," Ruby said with a knowing smile. She and Cece exchanged a look then glanced away.

"All of the decorations are looking especially fine, I agree," Cece said. "So, Sherry, what are you and Rusty doing for the holiday this year?"

"Are you exchanging gifts?" Ruby said.

Both women were grinning now. Sherry had the distinct impression they knew something she didn't and were enjoying holding something over on her.

"What is going on here?" she asked.

Neither woman would look at her directly, but Cece chuckled then pointed to her meal. "Are you done? Let's go shop some more."

By the time Sherry met Rusty for dinner, the ladies had convinced her to buy a sparkling white dress, matching shoes, and a nice coat with a faux fur collar that was definitely warm. Cece sprang for the pretty silk scarf that matched her dress, and Ruby had insisted on getting Sherry some perfume that reminded Sherry of the woods at night.

"You might want to wear those to dinner tonight," they both suggested. They were so nonchalant that Sherry knew there was more going on than they were saying, and she also knew that neither woman would spill their secrets without a lot more effort than she had to put into discovering what they were hiding.

Sherry looked at her friends suspiciously, but they both pretended not to notice her scrutiny.

As they left the herb shop after dropping off Ruby, Cece introduced Sherry to a tourist.

"This is Reverend Foster. He's visiting here with a youth group staying at the inn. Reverend Foster, this is Sherry Grimes."

"Well, hello, Sherry. My pleasure. Hey, you're Rusty's girl, aren't you?" He was a large man with a huge smile and bigger belly that resembled a certain jolly winter fellow children loved to have visit them.

Sherry shook his hand and returned the pleasantries. "Yes, I'm with him. You know him? How long are you visiting with us, Reverend?" she asked politely.

"Yes, I've known Rusty a long time. He's a good man. And we're here until the day after Christmas. Our group comes every year. We love the skiing here."

"Yes, we do get awesome snowfall on the mountains. Are you from around here?" Sherry asked.

"Oh, from a little farther up north of here. Well, very nice to meet you. I'm sure we'll be seeing you again." He nodded his goodbyes and left with a woman Sherry assumed was his wife.

"He seems very nice," Sherry said to Cece as they crossed the square toward the music shop. She watched the reverend and his wife enter the new toy shop next door to Cece's store and shook her head. As much as that man resembled Santa, she was even surer it could totally be possible when a group of small children in bright colored caps and sweaters followed the couple into the store.

"Oh, yes, he's very sweet," Cece agreed. She was chuckling. "I have to get back to the shop and close up. Have a nice dinner with Rusty."

"Yes, thanks. See you later."

Sherry strolled down the street. Her new dress felt silky, and she was glad she'd agreed to purchase it. Around her, the crowds ebbed and flowed. When she reached Napoli's, she stepped inside and into a winter wonderland. They'd really done up the decorations for the holidays. Red, green, and gold were everywhere. Strands of sparkling white lights twinkled from the ceiling and on the tables. The red checked tablecloths were crisp, and on the tables were small green wreaths with candles lit merrily in their centers.

Sherry, her attention drawn to the pretty lights, smiled at the waitress standing at her elbow, clearing her throat. She held a menu in her hand and motioned Sherry into the restaurant.

"I wasn't even sure if you would be open tonight on Christmas Eve, but Rusty insisted you would be." She turned at the sound of a familiar voice calling her. That's when she noticed the restaurant was empty except for them. That was strange. Napoli's was very popular and if open, should be packed.

"Sherry, over here." Rusty stood up and waved her over to their table.

She walked between the tables to his side and kissed him with more enthusiasm than usual. Something about this whole evening was feeling magical. Rusty had changed from his flannel, jeans, and hiking boots to a nice shirt with a tie and black pants that looked suspiciously new. She had a feeling she wasn't the only one who'd gone shopping today.

She noticed a bottle of champagne in a bucket of ice on the table.

Rusty looked nervous. Blushing when she looked at him, he lowered his eyes to the menu.

Sherry reached out and touched his hand.

"Rusty, I have something to tell you, and I'm not sure how to say this." She couldn't keep the tremor out of her voice ,and he jerked up to look at her with fear in his eyes. His whole body stiffened at her words, and she hurried to reassure him she wasn't giving him bad news. "Actually, it might be good news."

"Oh?" he said. He stared into her eyes as if trying to force the words out of her. He set the menu down and gave her his undivided attention, and she couldn't help but notice he'd paled.

"You know I love you, right?"

"I thought you did," he said. A muscle twitched along his jaw as if he was clenching his teeth.

"I do. I really do, but . . ." Sherry tore her gaze away from his, not sure how to tell him what she'd done. Hoping when she did tell him that he wouldn't hate her. How would he feel knowing she'd written their love story for the whole world to read? Would he tell her to leave?

"But . . . ?" He motioned the waitress off.

"I . . . you know I've been writing, right?" She wished she could just blurt out what she'd done, but she needed to find a way to make him see that it was good for both of them. But would he see it that way?

"Yes, so?" Now he looked confused.

She reached out and touched his hand. "I wrote a love story based on us called Heartwood Glen. I sent it to some agents, and I heard back yesterday that one wanted to represent me, and so I sent back a contract." There. The band-aid was ripped off.

Sherry held her breath, waiting for Rusty to react. She lowered her eyes, afraid to look at him.

It started with a low rumble, then a louder growl, then an outright guffaw. Two minutes later, they were both laughing, but Sherry had no idea why.

Rusty took her hand in his and said, his voice serious, "I thought you were breaking up with me. I thought you didn't love me anymore."

"What?" Sherry said, squeezing his hand. "I love you with all my heart, Rusty. I couldn't love anyone else the way I love you. Why would you think I was leaving you?"

"I've been so worried about this," he muttered. He fumbled in his pants pocket.

"About . . . ?"

Suddenly, Rusty got down on one knee and pulled the box from his pocket with a flourish.

Staring deeply into her eyes, he said, while she held her breath in shock, "Will you marry me, Sherry, and complete my heart? Will you take me as I am to be your soul mate, forever bonded to you?"

Behind her, Sherry heard gasps and whispers around them. She glanced about and grinned to realize Cece, Ruby, and all her Havenwood Falls friends had come into the restaurant, watching her.

Turning her attention back to Rusty, she nodded her head, suddenly at a loss for words.

"Yes," she finally was able to get out.

Rusty slipped the ring on her finger and followed the motion with a lean into her embrace and a kiss that struck her very core with its certainty that this was the absolute right answer.

A short time later, just as the clock struck midnight, Reverend Foster asked her if she would take this man as her husband, and standing there in her new shimmery white dress, under the mistletoe in the gazebo with the town's most important people around her, she said yes.

She promised her love to the man who'd won her heart all those years ago in the woods. "I will love you until the stars sink into the moon, until the sun forgets to shine, until my heart can no longer bear to be without its matching beat. I will be yours now, forever, and into eternity. When my body is no more, my heart will always be yours."

Rusty gazed back into her eyes and said, "And I will love you until the moon howls for me. I will love you even when I cannot hold you in my arms, but forever in my heart. I will never forsake you or forget you. You are my heart, my breath, my existence."

Together they said, as their friends cheered around them, "My heart will only beat for you in this life, and in all lives."

And later, when they were finally alone in their bed, Rusty proved to Sherry just what forever meant.

Read Sherry and Rusty's story in *Old Wounds* by Susan Burdorf

THE PERFECT GIFT

BY ROSE GARCIA

A Joe & Infiniti Short Story

Joe paced the floor of his bedroom while his best friend, Kase, stared at him. His eyes were wide, his mouth slightly parted. He rubbed the back of his neck.

"Uh . . ." Kase finally said. "You want to what?"

Joe knew it sounded crazy, but he loved Infiniti. He was called to her, which meant he was bound to her for life. Mated forever. He thought for sure Kase would understand. They were in the same wolf pack. They grew up together. They were even together when they found Infiniti after her car crashed outside Havenwood Falls.

Joe sat on the edge of his bed. He rubbed his palms on his jeans. "I want to ask Infiniti to marry me."

A long silence hovered in the air before Kase uttered, "That's what I thought you said."

Joe ran his fingers through his short blond hair. "We won't get married anytime soon, but I want to take that next step with her. You know, be official and give her something to symbolize our bond."

"I get that. I really do. But, dude, marriage?"

Kase was with Elle, but they were only dating. Nothing more. So Kase had no idea what it was like to be called to someone. Maybe if he had, his reaction would be different. So instead of getting into it with his friend, Joe dropped the subject.

"You know what, forget it." Joe grabbed his duffle bag with his gym clothes. "Come on. Let's go workout."

Kase slung his bag over his shoulder, looking relieved. "Yeah, let's go. We can talk about this whole thing later."

Pumping iron at the gym, Kase kept the conversation on football. Joe did his best to stay interested in the discussion about the Denver Broncos and their offensive line, but his mind kept drifting to Infiniti, who was hanging out with her best friend Taylor for the day. He and Infiniti had their first date almost exactly a year ago. He took her to the Cold Moon Ball. Joe still remembered how amazing she looked in her purple dress. He also remembered how she had been attacked that night by the wild wolf pack on the back patio of the Mills Mansion and later how they had shared their first kiss at Howe's Herbal Shoppe.

Ever since then, it seemed as if he had to fight every supernatural force in existence to be with her. He'd gone from finding her at the crash, to losing her to a time jump, to saving her when she reappeared in Havenwood Falls, to losing her to another time jump, and then to finding her in the past and bringing her to his timeline permanently. And then, they had barely survived their first semester at Sun & Moon Academy Halvard Campus. He was beginning to think their time together was limited. And if that was the case, he wanted to be bonded to her in every way possible before something else happened.

"Uh, dude?"

Kase was laying on his back on the workbench, staring up at Joe, about to lift a barbell loaded with weights on each end. "Care to spot me?"

Joe snapped to attention. "Yep, sorry."

After about an hour of reps, and with Joe's thoughts still on Infiniti, he and Kase finally finished. They headed to Burger Bar for their usual post-workout double bacon cheeseburgers.

When they got there, they found the place packed. Holiday music blared over the lively conversations in the restaurant. Twinkling lights and Christmas decorations adorned every nook and cranny. They scooted their way through the crowd and scored two seats at the counter. Even though Joe knew what he wanted, he took a menu anyway. Sometimes the restaurant offered seasonal specials.

"All right," Kase said, turning to face his friend. "Just do it."

Joe lowered his menu. "Huh?"

"Propose to Fin so you can go back to being normal."

"Really?"

"Yes, really," Kase said with an exasperated laugh. "I mean, you are mated, so why not?"

Excitement sparked inside of Joe. He clapped Kase on the back. "Thanks, dude.

Joe and Kase laughed and joked while devouring their meals. And Joe was pumped. He was going to do it. He was going to propose to Infiniti. Now all he needed to do was figure out the specifics and tell his parents.

With her arms weighed down with shopping bags, Infiniti shook the snow off her shoulders as she walked into the crowded and lively Coffee Haven with her best friend, Taylor. The welcoming warmth of the heated coffee shop wrapped around her cold body as the aroma of freshly brewed coffee filled her lungs.

"Hey, guys!" It was Harlow, Taylor's sister. She was working the busy counter and motioned for them to get in line.

"Wow," Infiniti said, over the holiday music. "It's packed."

"Yep," Taylor said. "It's always crazy-busy like this over the holidays."

When they got to the front of the line, Infiniti ordered a caramel macchiato and Taylor ordered a Witch's Brew latte.

"I'll call your names when it's ready," Harlow said, taking their payment. A group got up and started to leave the shop. Harlow pointed quickly. "Hurry! Go snag that table!"

Infiniti and Taylor made a beeline for the back of the shop and slid into the newly vacant booth. Infiniti unloaded her things beside her then eyed her shopping bags. She'd spent the day shopping with Taylor and still hadn't figured out what to get Joe for Christmas. After everything they'd been through and how much they loved each other, a sweater and cologne for the guy she wanted to be with forever didn't seem like enough. And then she thought of how they'd been together for a year now and went out on their first date last year at the Cold Moon Ball.

Taylor wrinkled her face in an expression of curiosity. The movement caused the light over the table to reflect against the diamond stud on the left side of her small nose.

"What are you thinking, Fin? You look a million miles away."

Infiniti leaned over the table. "When's the Cold Moon Ball?"

"It was last week, on December 12th. We were still at SMA. Why?"

Her shoulders slumped. "I thought I could maybe give Joe an early gift and tie it in with the ball."

"Why the Cold Moon Ball?"

"That was my and Joe's first date last year." Infiniti's mind went back to that night. She remembered walking into the spectacular Mills Mansion with the massive skylight overhead and crystal candelabras everywhere. "I fell in love with Joe that night. Like, really fell in love with him. In this incredible holiday town mixed with supernatural dangers and science fiction realities, I found my person."

The cheerful holiday tune slowed to a romantic melody. The twinkling lights outside the windows showcased a dazzling snowfall. And Infiniti's heart swelled with love for Joe.

"Wow," Taylor sighed. "It's like you're living your own Hallmark movie."

"Well, you are too!"

Taylor rested her chin in her hand, and Infiniti could tell she was thinking of Clay.

"You're right," Taylor admitted. "What Clay and I have is pretty amazing, and I think about him all the time now that he's home in Maine for the holidays, but we haven't been dating that long. We're nowhere near where you and Joe are."

Harlow swooped in with a tray of two mugs of coffee adorned with Christmas tree shaped cream. "Geez, didn't you hear me calling your names?"

"Oops, no. Sorry!" Taylor offered.

Harlow handed over the concoctions, then set down a small plate of sugar cookies. "And these are on the house."

"Thanks, Harlow," Infiniti and Taylor said in unison.

"You're welcome." She started back for the counter but paused and said over her shoulder, "Let me know if you guys need anything else."

Infiniti picked up her mug then blew on it before resting her lips on the rim and taking a sip. The warm mocha goodness slid down her throat while she thought of what she could get for Joe. Still coming up short on ideas, she groaned. "Shopping for guys is hard."

"You got that right. Especially when you're in love." But then Taylor perked up. "Unless you give the ultimate gift!"

"Huh?"

Taylor moved in, as if she was about to let Infiniti in on a huge secret. "Sex," she whispered.

Infiniti's mouth fell open. She hadn't expected that out of her best friend, but then again, it kinda made sense. She had decided back when she was facing her hourglass challenge at SMA that she wanted to give herself to Joe completely. That he'd be her first and her last. But every time they got close, they were interrupted.

"Well?" Taylor prodded.

"Well," Infiniti said in a low voice, "I'm definitely ready, but we haven't exactly found the right time or place. And even though doing it in front of a romantic fireplace over the holidays sounds ideal, how would we pull that off? Joe lives at home, and I'm staying with Lyra Beaumont. We're not even old enough to rent a room or anything."

"Fine, home for the holidays won't work. But you can maybe promise yourself to him somehow? And plan something special when you guys get back to school? Maybe give him a sexy nightie and a love note?"

A surge of excitement followed by embarrassment filled Infiniti. "I don't know. Maybe?"

Taylor giggled. "Well, you'll think of something."

The two spent the next hour chatting and laughing. And even though the conversation was lively, Infiniti kept thinking of Joe and what she could possibly get him for Christmas. Surely something would come to her.

Joe headed straight for the shower when he got home from Burger Bar. Lathering up under the hot stream, he thought of what he would say to his mom and dad about his plan to propose to Infiniti for Christmas. He knew his parents were crazy about her, but he wasn't sure how they'd feel about him proposing. Even though he was called to Infiniti, he wondered if his parents would be okay with an engagement so soon into their relationship, especially since they were both in their first year of college. But then again, he was a wolf shifter. She was a transhuman with newfound supernatural powers. Nothing about their relationship was exactly normal.

When he finished, he yanked the towel off the towel rack and started drying off. A pounding sounded on the bathroom door.

"Joe!" It was Joe's little brother, Boris. He was fourteen but acted like he was twelve. "I've got the game all set up!"

Boris had been complaining about his big brother spending all of his time with Infiniti, so Joe had planned to spend the evening with his little brother. He wrapped his towel around his waist and opened the door.

"What game?"

Boris was almost an exact replica of Joe with blond hair and hazel eyes. Except where Joe was tall and muscular, Boris was short and stocky. He still hadn't hit a big growth spurt.

"It's a new game I got as an early Christmas present called Fight to the Death!"

Joe laughed as he headed for his room. "Fight to the Death? Sounds like a game you're gonna lose, bro."

Boris pushed Joe's back. "You wish. Now hurry up. I'll be in the living room."

Joe slipped on a T-shirt and some sweatpants. He picked up his phone to see if Infiniti had texted, but she hadn't. He tried resisting the urge to send her a message, but couldn't help himself.

ME: Hey, thinking of you

Not two seconds later, three little dots appeared on Joe's screen, letting him know Infiniti was texting back.

INFINITI: Sameeee

Even though he was with her the day before, and would see her in the morning, he could never get enough of her.

ME: What time should I come get you in the morning

INFINITI: As early as possible. Actually, I want to sleep in, lol How's noon

ME: Noon is good. Gonna play a game with Boris now

INFINITI: Ok, love you

ME: Love you

Joe joined his family in the living room. Boris was sitting on the floor, game on, controllers at the ready. Their mom bustled about in the kitchen, whipping up her famous *fritule* dessert, a Croatian dish that was like a donut but way better. Their dad was kicked back on his recliner, reading a book. Since everyone was together, Joe thought it was the perfect time to tell them his plan to propose to Infiniti.

"Um, everyone, I have an announcement."

Joe's mom came closer. Flour dusted her forehead, and her arm wrapped around her mixing bowl. His dad lowered his book to just below eye level. Boris flashed Joe a look of irritation.

"What's up, son?" his mom asked.

"Well, you guys know how I feel about Infiniti. And how I'm bound to her and how she's equally attached to me."

Joe's mom had been stirring the contents of her bowl, but stopped. His dad folded the book closed and set it on his lap. Boris perked up, catching on that something important was about to be discussed.

"Well . . ." Joe rubbed his hands together. "Infiniti is—"

"Pregnant!" Boris called out.

Joe grabbed the nearest couch cushion and chucked it at his brother. "Boris!"

Boris laughed, but when he saw the look of anger on Joe's face, he stopped. "Sorry."

Joe turned away from his brother and focused on his parents. "What I was going to say is that Infiniti is the most important person in my life, and I don't ever want to be away from her. And so," he blew out, " I've decided to ask her to marry me on Christmas Eve."

The fire crackled and popped in the fireplace while everyone stood in silence for a while.

"And no," Joe added right away, giving Boris the side eye. "She's not pregnant."

Joe's mom set her bowl on the coffee table. She wiped her hands on the kitchen towel draped over her shoulder and pushed her long blond hair behind her ears. She went over to Joe's dad, who was now on his feet. And then his mom smiled. And when she did, Joe started breathing again, not even realizing he'd been holding his breath.

"Oh, son," his mom said. "We are thrilled that you've found your one true mate and that it's someone as lovely and wonderful as Infiniti."

"We couldn't have picked a better mate for you," his dad chimed in.

"She's all right," Boris said with a laugh before punching Joe on the shoulder.

"Boris," Mom scolded. "Enough." She brought Joe in for a hug and held him for a while. Then she pulled back and cupped his face with her hands. "Well, I guess you'll be needing the ring. I'll be right back."

When she left the room, his dad moved in and clasped his arm. "You do mean for a long engagement. Right, son?"

"Uh, yeah. We won't get married until we're finished with school." Joe raised his eyebrow. "Dad, what ring?"

"Your mom will explain."

After a few minutes, his mom came back into the room with a

small red box in her hand. She took a seat on the couch and motioned for Joe to sit next to her.

"When your father and I met, we fell hard for each other, much like you and Infiniti."

"It's the wolf thing." His dad winked.

"We weren't much older than you when we got engaged," his mom said. She held out her left hand, showing Joe her wedding ring—a round diamond surrounded by two bands of sapphires.

"This engagement ring came from your dad's mom," she explained. "It's been passed down for generations." She held up the red box. "And this ring is from my mom. It too has been passed down for generations." She extended the box to Joe. "Now, it's yours."

Joe had planned on using his savings to buy Infiniti a ring. He figured it wouldn't be that big, but had told himself he could upgrade it later. But now, he had an heirloom to offer. He took the box and opened it. Inside sparkled the most perfect elongated diamond he'd ever seen.

"Wow, Mom and Dad. It's perfect. Thank you so much."

"The shape is called marquise. And I think it'll look amazing on Infiniti," his mom said with a huge smile on her face.

"What if she says no?" Boris asked.

His dad swatted Boris on the back of his head with a whack. "Enough out of you, young man."

Joe ignored his brother, gave his parents a group hug, then went to his room to put the ring away. Back in the living room, everyone had returned to what they were doing. Mom was baking, Dad was reading, and Boris was on the floor. Diving into the shoot-em-up game with his little brother, Joe couldn't suppress the nagging doubt creeping in his mind. Boris had a good point. What if he was asking Infiniti to marry him too soon? What if she said no?

When Infiniti got back to Lyra's house after Coffee Haven, she took off her coat, hat, and gloves in the foyer and hung them on the hooks. She slid off her black boots.

"Lyra! I'm back!"

With no answer, she hauled her shopping bags to her room and emptied the contents onto her bed. She eyed the glittery silver and gold wrapping supplies, then smiled at the gifts, proud of her purchases. She got Lyra a super soft scarf with the most amazing purple and gold colors complete with matching ear muffs. She got Joe's mom a set of dish towels and hot pads monogrammed with a *G* for Greg in big red cursive writing. For Joe's dad, she got a tactical flashlight that turned on with a crank instead of batteries, perfect for his late night patrol duties. And for Boris, she got a wireless camouflage speaker. All she needed was a gift for Taylor and something special for Joe.

She had planned on spending the next day with Joe and could drag him with her to go shopping for Taylor's gift. And, of course, she could eye the options for Joe while they were out. There had to be something special for him, something to let him know how deeply she loved him.

Lost in ideas of what to get him, Infiniti suddenly realized how quiet the house was. A blast of icy panic overcame her as the all too familiar feeling of being in danger set in. She was always around people at SMA. But now, back in Havenwood Falls for the holidays, she had moments of aloneness. And every time she was by herself, she kind of freaked out, envisioning all kinds of murderous creatures coming to get her.

"Okay," she said to herself, resisting the urge to text Joe or Taylor. She needed to overcome her fears on her own the way Dr. Lavinia had taught her back at school. "No one is after me. I'm just alone in this cozy and safe house. There's no danger here."

A weak laugh escaped her lips, filling the emptiness in the room. Clearly, reassuring self-talk wasn't enough. She reached for her phone and opened up her playlist. Music started pouring out of the speaker on her bedside table. She sat on her bed and focused on the tune.

Singing along and getting caught up in the beat, her fears started melting away.

"Yep, I got this," she mumbled to herself.

She sorted through the stuff on her bed and got to work wrapping the gifts. Trying to make everything look as pretty as possible, but having a really hard time, she thought of her mom's horrible gift-wrapping skills. A lone tear escaped her eye, and she wiped it away quickly. Even though Taylor had used her skills to help her say goodbye to her mom in the spirit world, she still missed her something awful.

She held up her handiwork as if her mom could see. "Not bad, huh?"

Pulling herself together, she continued with her task until she was finished. Pleased with her efforts, she gathered up the treasures, went to the living room, and placed them under the Christmas tree.

Before she could slip into another bout of sadness, the back door opened.

"Lyra?"

"It's me!"

Infiniti went through the kitchen to the backdoor and found Lyra struggling with armloads of groceries bags. Infiniti went to her right away and helped her with the load. They piled the sacks on the counter and started putting everything away. Then they threw together a quick late dinner of pasta salad.

Sitting across the kitchen table from one of the most powerful witches in town, Infiniti chatted with her hostess about their day while they ate. Infiniti couldn't help but think how lucky she was to have been taken in by such an amazing woman. Even though she had enough money from her mom's life insurance policy to get a small place in town, Lyra wouldn't have it. She gladly opened her home to Infiniti for breaks and summers while she was in college, telling Infiniti to save her money and get a place after she graduated. At first, Infiniti felt bad about imposing, but then she welcomed having a home with a motherly figure.

"What is it, Infiniti?"

Infiniti smiled. "I'm just really grateful for you. That's all."

Lyra reached out and took Infiniti's hand. She squeezed. "And I you."

After dinner, and with everything cleaned up, Infiniti got ready for bed. Showered and getting tired, she snuggled under the covers with her earbuds on. She was dying to hear from Joe but didn't want to bug him. A text flashed on her phone.

JOE: Hey, babe
ME: Hey
JOE: What are you doing?
ME: In bed, thinking of you
JOE: Wish I was there

A flurry of butterflies exploded in her stomach, and her cheeks flushed. She'd give anything to have Joe in bed with her, touching her, kissing her, and doing all the things that made her tingle. But mostly, just holding her.

JOE: I'm gonna call you

Her phone rang, and she answered right away.

"I had to hear your voice," Joe said, sounding oh-so-sexy.

They talked through the night, and somewhere between longing for Joe and craving him, she fell asleep.

Infiniti practically sprang out of bed the next day, eager to spend time with her man. She dressed in her black skinny jeans and a comfy blue sweater. With her makeup in place and her long, wavy brown hair fluffed, she headed for the kitchen and found Lyra on her laptop.

"You heading out?" she asked Infiniti.

"Yeah, gonna finish my shopping and hang with Joe."

Infiniti started munching on a granola bar when the doorbell rang. It was exactly noon, and Joe was right on time.

"See you later, Lyra!"

"Have fun!"

The day was cold, but not overly. Hand in hand, she and Joe

strolled along Main Street where all the shops were. She found the perfect hardbound journal for Taylor with sparkling stars and a crescent moon embossed on the front cover. She even got the matching candle scented with vetiver, smoke, and spruce. She knew Taylor would love it. And then, while continuing their loop of the square, she spotted Summit Jewelers on the corner of Eighth and Main. She thought they might have some cool gems and definitely wanted to go in.

Making their way around the shop, she peered at the wall-to-wall glass cases that housed the most amazing sparkling jewels. As she was eyeing everything, she spotted a case of men's leather bracelets. Trying not to let Joe catch on to her interest, she casually passed the case but kept her gaze on a piece in the center. It was a multi-strand dark leather bracelet with a stainless steel clasp on the front that could easily be engraved. That was it. The perfect gift for Joe.

Now, she needed to get rid of him so she could order it. She tugged him to the exit, and they stepped out on the sidewalk. The temperature hadn't changed, but Infiniti faked a hard shiver as if the temperature had suddenly dropped.

"You okay?"

"Yeah, I'm good. It just feels a lot colder out here."

Joe put his arm around her and rubbed her arms. "That better?"

His warm embrace felt great, but she needed to get rid of him for a few minutes. "Yes, but . . . do you mind going to the car and getting my hat? I left it on my seat, I think."

He paused for a second. "Yeah, sure thing."

She pointed over her shoulder to the jewelry store. "I'll wait in here where it's warm."

He kissed her lips. "Be right back."

She went back into the store and headed straight for the men's bracelets and bought the one that had caught her eye. And luckily for her, they could have it engraved in time for Christmas Eve.

"What do you want it to say?" the store clerk asked.

"Forever Yours. And then, under that and centered, can you put an infinity symbol?"

The clerk drew it out on a piece of paper for her approval, and it looked perfect. She paid and stepped away from the counter just as Joe walked in. She hurried over to him, took the hat he was holding, and pulled him outside.

"Where to next?" she asked, giving him a peck on the lips and putting the hat on.

"Wherever you want."

They were together for the rest of the day and every day after until it was finally Christmas Eve. Infiniti couldn't wait to spend the holiday with Joe and his family. And she was especially couldn't excited to give Joe his present.

Joe spent the day mostly in silence as he rehearsed in his mind over and over how he was going to propose to Infiniti later that evening. He planned on taking her driving around to look at Christmas lights after dinner. They'd end up at the square, which would be all set up for Rusty's last-minute wedding. He thought it'd be the perfect backdrop for a proposal. He had filled in everyone on his plan so they could be on the same page, but he was still so nervous. He worried that something would go wrong. He also worried she'd say no.

"You've been awful quiet today, son. Everything okay?" his mom asked when he came into the kitchen.

"I'm a little anxious, I guess. I want everything to be perfect."

She patted his arm. "It will be."

Joe eyed the busy kitchen, suddenly becoming aware of the delicious aroma of turkey in the oven. "You need any help in here?"

"Actually, with your dad out on patrol right now, I could use a hand." She pointed at the oven. "The turkey's been cooking for a while, and I don't put in the lamb until later. Wanna help with the sarma and peppers?"

"Sure."

Joe loved the traditional Croatian dishes they had at Christmas and couldn't wait to share that part of his heritage with Infiniti. He hoped she'd like the sarma, which was minced meat wrapped in cabbage, and the peppers, which were also stuffed with minced meat. And, of course, they'd have green beans and mashed potatoes.

He washed his hands and got to work. Even Boris came in and started helping. After a few hours, everything was finished. All that was left was for Joe to shower, get dressed in his dark navy suit, and pick up Infiniti. And when he got to Lyra's and Infiniti opened the door, his heart melted. She was wearing a green lace mini dress that hugged her body in all the right places while her long dark hair tumbled perfectly over her shoulders.

"Is this dress okay for the wedding?" she asked. She touched her fingers to that perfect spot at the base of her throat.

"Babe, it's more than okay." He glanced over her shoulder. "Is Lyra home?"

"No, she—"

Before Infiniti could finish her sentence, Joe stepped in and shut the door behind him. He wrapped one arm around her small waist and pulled her close. "I have to kiss you. Right. Now."

Infiniti's lips parted as she looked up at him. "Then kiss me," she breathed out. "Right. Now."

With a soft moan, he brushed his lips back and forth against hers, then kissed her long and deep, their tongues swirling together as his head soared in the clouds. After a while, he slowly pulled away.

"Wow," she whispered. "Joe, every time you kiss me is like the first time. You take my breath away."

In that moment, he didn't want to wait until after dinner to propose. He wanted to be bound to her in every way possible right then and there.

"Infiniti, I want to ask you something." He moved his hand to his coat pocket. He reached for the ring, but didn't feel it. Panic filled him. He dug his hand in further and poked around when his fingers scraped against a small hole in the corner of his pocket.

"Shit," he muttered.

Infiniti's brows stitched together. "What is it?"

"I, um . . ." He pulled his hand out. Even though he knew he'd put the ring in his right pocket, he checked the left one anyway. But the only thing in there were his keys. He pulled them out. "I um . . ." He scrambled for an excuse. "I thought I lost my keys." He let out a nervous laugh. "But here they are!"

"Oh," she said. "Yep, there they are. So . . . what did you want to ask me?"

His mind raced in a million different directions while he quickly retraced his steps. He put on his coat in his room, took the ring out of the red box, and placed it in his pocket. Then he went to the kitchen, out to his car, and straight to Lyra's. So somewhere between his room and Lyra's front door, he lost the heirloom diamond ring he wanted to give Infiniti.

He needed to figure out something, and quick. "Can I use the restroom?"

Infiniti looked surprised but mostly confused. "Um, sure." She stepped aside. "You know where it is."

"I'll be right back."

Alone in the restroom, he searched his pockets one more time and still came up empty. He wondered if there was someone he could call for help, when Taylor sprang to mind. She was a witch. Maybe she had an idea. He didn't have time for a long text, so he turned on the sink faucet full blast and called her.

"Joe?"

"Yeah, it's me," he said in a half-whisper. "I need your help."

"Oh my goddess," she whispered back. "Is it Fin? Is she okay? Are you okay?"

"Yeah, yeah, yeah. She's fine. We're both fine. But I lost her ring."

"Her ring?"

He didn't want to keep Infiniti waiting, so he hurried with his explanation. "I was going to propose to her tonight, but I lost the ring, and I need you to help me find it. Right now. Please."

Taylor paused. "You're going to propose?"

"Can you please focus, Taylor?"

"Shit, okay. Where are you?"

"I'm at Lyra's, picking up Infiniti. But we're heading to my house."

"Okay, I'll meet you at your place."

"But, Taylor, Infiniti can't know."

"I know. I get it. I'll text you when I'm there. I'll just need something the ring has touched."

"I have the ring box."

"Perfect. See you in a few."

Joe turned off the faucet, blew out, then went back to Infiniti. Worry covered her expression when she saw him.

"Are you okay?"

Joe laughed, trying his best to act as normal as possible. "I'm fine. Can't a guy go to the restroom?"

"Of course, but—"

"But now let's go," he said with a smile. "A traditional Croatian Christmas dinner awaits." He spotted a bag by the front door filled with wrapped gifts. "Are you bringing this?"

"Yep, these are for you and your family."

"Nice." He smiled. "Now let's get out of here."

"Wait," she said. "Were you going to ask me something?"

"Oh, yeah." He paused. "I was going to ask if you . . . knew how much I loved you. Now let's go. I'm hungry."

He took the bag in one hand and Infiniti's hand in the other, and practically dragged her out of the house so he could beat Taylor home.

Joe's family greeted Infiniti in their overly eager fashion—as if Infiniti was the last girl in the world and Joe had never dated before. And really, he never actually had. But his parents and Boris didn't need to act like it. They gathered around her, all smiles, asking her a million questions. Normally he would've intervened and saved her, but his phone vibrated. He knew it was Taylor.

"I'll be right back," he said, then headed for his room while he checked his message.

TAYLOR: I'm here, outside your bedroom window

He ducked into his room, locked the door, then opened his window. Taylor crawled in with a gust of cold and piles of snow on her head and shoulders. She shook herself free of the snowflakes.

"You owe me one, Joe."

"If you can find the ring, I'll owe you more than one." He took the red box from his dresser and handed it to her. "Now what?"

She held the box in one hand, then motioned for Joe to take her other one. "Focus on when you last remember having the ring, okay?"

Joe nodded. He pictured himself putting the ring in his pocket. "Got it."

"Good. Now close your eyes and chant with me."

Joe nodded again, then closed his eyes.

Taylor started whispering, "What was lost is now found. What was lost is now found."

Joe joined in, and together they repeated the phrase over and over until Taylor stopped. She squeezed Joe's hand in a death grip.

"I see it."

Joe peeked at her. "Where?"

Her eyes were still shut tight. "Wow, it's so pretty, Joe!"

"Taylor!"

"Sorry," she said. "I see it nestled in something plushy and blue. Like, a sweater? Or a blanket?"

"My bath mat?"

Taylor's eyes snapped open. "You lost Fin's engagement ring in the bathroom?"

Joe shushed her so the others wouldn't hear. "If your skills are accurate, then yes."

And then Taylor laughed. "This is a good story for later."

"Much later. Thanks, Taylor."

He opened the window, helped her climb back out, and hurried to the bathroom. He crouched down on all fours and patted the bath mat. Sure enough, the ring was nestled deep in the fibers. With a sigh of relief, he plucked it out. He polished it off, slipped it in the pocket with *no* holes, then joined the others in the dining room.

For the next few hours, Joe, his family, and Infiniti enjoyed the most amazing dinner. And Infiniti delighted in trying the Croatian fare while his mom explained each dish. When they finished, everyone cleared the table so they could have coffee and *fritule* while they played a game of charades. It was the best Christmas Joe had ever had, and as everything was winding down and with plenty of time before they had to leave for Rusty's wedding, he activated his plan.

"I was thinking I'd take Infiniti around town to see the lights before we open our gifts," he announced.

"Oh, yeah, let's go!" Boris exclaimed.

Joe widened his eyes at him and cleared his throat, irritated that Boris had forgotten the plan.

"Boris, I need you here with me and Dad to help out in the kitchen," his mom said, poking him playfully in the ribs.

"But, Mom," Boris complained. He started to say something else when a look of recognition set in. "Oh, yeah, that's right. I need to stay here."

"It's okay with me if Boris comes along," Infiniti offered.

"Nah, that's okay, Fin. I . . . love . . . cleaning . . . the kitchen."

Joe took Infiniti's hand before Boris could say anything else.

"We won't be long," he called out, leading her to the foyer and draping her coat over her shoulders.

Alone at last in the car, they chatted about their evening while driving around and admiring the spectacular lights on just about every structure in Havenwood Falls. And when they got close to the square, Joe parked the car. A host of nerves swirled inside him. Would Infiniti say yes to his proposal? Was she ready to be engaged? Or was it all too soon? He was starting to second guess himself.

Infiniti reached out and started playing with his fingers. "What are we doing here?"

He leaned his head against the headrest and took her in—long dark hair, perfect porcelain skin, big brown eyes. She was the most beautiful woman in the world, and he could stare at her forever. "I thought we could walk around the square."

Bundled up and huddled close together, they strolled down Main Street. And when they got to the square, Infiniti sucked in her breath.

"Wow," she muttered.

Christmas decorations lit up the square as usual. But this time, the oversized gazebo was all decked out for Rusty's wedding. Flowing white fabric draped the poles of the structure. Lights and greenery circled all around. With the snowflakes sprinkling down from the sky, the scene looked straight out of a fairy tale.

"Joe, this is magical." She held him tight.

He squeezed her hand. "Let's go take a closer look."

They made their way to the magnificent gazebo and stood in the center. Infiniti looked up, and Joe followed her line of sight to a bundle of mistletoe hanging down from a white lace ribbon. Joe smiled and looked down at Infiniti.

"You have to kiss me," she said with a smile, her nose red from the cold.

"Yes, I do. But first, I want to tell you something."

He stepped back and took her hands in his. "Infiniti Clausman, from the moment you crashed into my world, my life hasn't been the same. You are a beaming light in the darkest night, and your spirit has opened up my heart to a love and a joy I didn't know existed. I want you by my side, forever. In all the good and all the bad and all the near-death situations and all the crazy challenges, I want to face everything with you. You have filled my heart and my soul, and I love you, Infiniti. I love you beyond what love even is." He lowered himself to one knee, pulled the ring out of his pocket, and held it up to her. "Will you marry me?"

Infiniti's eyes watered over, and her lip quivered. She lowered herself to her knees in front of Joe while tears spilled from her eyes. She wrapped her hands around his.

"I love you, Joseph Greg. So much. And I never want to be without you. Not ever. So yes, I will marry you."

He wiped the tears from her face, then slipped the ring on her finger. Infiniti threw her arms around his neck as they kissed with love and passion.

Later that night, after the proposal and congratulatory champagne and gift opening with his family, followed by Rusty's midnight wedding, Joe took Infiniti back to Lyra's. He crawled into bed around three a.m., holding the bracelet Infiniti had given him. With his lamp still on, he eyed the inscription *Forever Yours* with an infinity symbol below. He was excited about being with Infiniti forever. He set the bracelet down on the bedside table then turned off the lamp. With the enveloping darkness, he thought of all the crap that had happened to them, especially at SMA. Turning on his side, he hoped the worst was behind them, and that their spring semester would be a semester of them exploring their love instead of fighting for survival. But somehow, he knew he'd probably be wrong.

Read Infiniti and Joe's story starting with *Saving Infiniti* and *Finding Infiniti* both by Rose Garcia, and continuing in *Sun & Moon Academy Book One: Fall Semester.*

DISCOVER THE MAGIC

BY BELINDA BORING

A Tempest & Natalie Short Story

Two things were becoming glaringly obvious.

First, I had learned nothing from the last time I'd come to one of Sedona's celebration dinners, and second, I should've worn my stretchy pants—fashion be damned.

Judging by the way my best friend, Natalie Putnam, was shifting about in her seat, she was having the same thoughts as me. Everything our gracious host had cooked for our Christmas Eve dinner had looked and tasted so delicious, it felt like a heinous crime to leave a single crumb behind on our plates.

Sedona was Micah Westbrook's girlfriend/hopefully soon to be fiancée. Honestly, I had no idea what was taking the guy so long to propose, but who knew when it came to old people.

Old. I wouldn't exactly label my favorite professor and mentor that but watching him with his family tonight had once again shown me how totally screwed up my own family had been. But that's a story for another time.

Right now, I was desperately trying not to burp and groan out loud. Goddess help me when it came time for dessert! All bets would be off when it came to manners.

"We have a surprise for you both," Sedona chimed in. She wore the biggest smile, and her eyes twinkled with mischief as she glanced over at Micah. "With it being your first Christmas in Havenwood Falls, we wanted to start a new tradition with you."

Micah reached over and grabbed hold of Sedona's hand, squeezing it affectionately. "It was actually Holly who came up with the idea."

There was that familiar expression of pride that I recognized the few times he leveled it at me during the semester. This time his attention was directed at his charge, Holly. She was a cute kid, and she positively beamed at his praise.

"It was nothing," she countered bashfully, squirming in her seat as she focused on her empty plate. Part of me wondered why she wasn't used to his compliments, but I knew from personal experience that even I doubted I'd ever become immune. There was just something so genuine and heartfelt about Mr. Westbrook. It was part of the reason why Natalie and I never refused an invitation to come visit.

They'd adopted us, and we'd gratefully accepted them as our newfound family.

"Let me go get it," Sedona said. Scooting back her chair, she disappeared into the kitchen. "Just give me a second."

I couldn't resist. Leaning forward, I locked eyes with Micah. "While I appreciate the effort, if I have to take one more mouth of whatever deliciousness she's about to bring in here, I'm gonna explode over everything." I gave him a no-nonsense nod as I sat back. "Consider yourself warned."

Natalie elbowed me sharply, hissing for me to shut up.

"Maybe Santa needs to bring you a book on guest etiquette." It was all said in fun, but there was no hiding the slight flicker of mortification that crossed her features. Even though we'd come by the house for a variety of reasons, my best friend and roommate was still a little hung up on the fact that we were good friends with one of the college's professors.

I blew out a short raspberry and snort. "I'm on his naughty list this year. All I'm expecting is a lump of coal on my altar."

She rolled her eyes at me. I replied with a self-deprecating shrug.

Holly watched on, chewing on her bottom lip like she was suddenly worried. "I hope you like the idea."

I hated the doubt I heard in her voice. From what I'd seen and heard, she was finally thriving here in town after being on the constant go—moving from place to place with Micah as her protector—and slowly making friends.

Which reminded me—I needed to have a little conversation with her about how she could count on me and Natalie as sisters. We'd try to be good influences on her . . . fingers crossed.

"They're going to love it, sweetheart," Sedona answered as she returned to the room. There was no holding back the moan of relief at not seeing a huge dish of dessert. I needed more time to digest and recover from the beef roast and fixings. Maybe I shouldn't have had that extra bread roll.

She didn't come back empty-handed, however.

"Did you want the honors, Holly?" Sedona held up a single sheet of paper.

The teen shook her head at first, but once she saw that we were all smiling at her, she seemed to relax and dropped the strand of hair she'd been fidgeting with.

"Well," she started, letting out a shaky breath. "I figured that even though you've been going to the Academy, you haven't really gotten a chance to experience Havenwood Falls yet. Especially at Christmas." Leaving her seat, Holly came around to where Natalie and I were sitting and presented us with the surprise. "So we came up with a scavenger hunt."

Color me intrigued.

Sure enough, that's exactly what the written poem stated, and without thinking, I began to read it out aloud.

It's your first Christmas with us
And we're so glad you're here.
We created this fun scavenger hunt
To fill you with festive cheer.

. . .

So off you go exploring,
The clues on this list your light.
And gather up each trinket,
Of what you find this night.

Make some brand-new memories,
Follow the way the sparkle calls.
Because your only goal is to discover
The magic of Havenwood Falls.

Holly was actually holding her breath.

Natalie beat me to the praise as she clapped her hands and threw her arms around Holly. "This is so thoughtful! Thank you!"

I knew how much this meant to my bestie because she was still struggling with her grief over her mother. I'd expected her to fall apart after her hourglass challenge and kind of disappear from society, but she'd shown unbelievable strength and grace. She wasn't lying that this meant something to her.

"I can't believe you did this for us," I chimed in, grinning like a fool. "When does it start? Please tell me now because Natalie and I have zero patience when it comes to waiting."

Micah mouthed *thank you* as he wrapped his arm around his charge. "That's the plan. You two bundle up, and while you're out, we'll finish preparing the second part to your surprise."

That stopped us both in our tracks. "There's more?" I shot a quick look at Holly. "You're not coming with us?"

Her brown hair waved as she shook her head happily. "Nope. I have more magic up my sleeve."

Taking that as her cue, Sedona began shooing us toward the door

133

as Holly raced ahead and started handing us our coats, scarves, and gloves. Micah came up from behind with his hands shoved into the front pockets of his blue jeans, his buffalo checkered shirt rolled up to his elbows.

"Have fun, girls!" he hollered.

"Be careful of snow drifts," Sedona added.

Holly was the last to speak as we were unceremoniously pushed out of the house. "And don't come back until you've completed your mission!"

The air held a brisk chill, and snowflakes lazily drifted down from the sky. It was typical December weather here in town, and for a brief moment, I felt a twinge of homesickness for New York City.

"Well," Natalie uttered, clouds of white forming from her breath. "At least they let us grab our stuff." She'd already wrapped her purple woolen scarf around her neck and was adjusting her fingers in a matching set of gloves. "Here, let me look at the list while you get ready."

Excitement fluttered inside my chest, and a lot of it was to do with the girl I was currently standing with. This was exactly what we needed to get into the Christmas spirit.

I pulled out the black slouch beanie from my pocket and tugged it down over my ears. "You figured out the first clue yet?"

Natalie beamed. "Easy peasy."

And off we went.

"Do you think they took pity on us and made the first one easy?"

I didn't drag my gaze away from the twinkling lights to answer Natalie. Instead, I shrugged.

"If so, it's hard to be offended when we're standing here dazzled. She seriously puts the Macy's Christmas window display to shame, that's for sure." My admission came out in a whisper. All I could think was *wow*!

Natalie read the first clue again.

. . .

First impressions matter,
Before you step inside.
When it comes to festive tradition,
This window displays that pride.

Snow and glitter, twinkling lights,
Where the theme surrounds a book.
But don't just stand there staring,
Come inside and take a look.

The moment we'd read the words *window display*, we knew exactly what direction to take. Sedona's bookstore, Shelf Indulgence, was always the talk of the town because she enjoyed creating fun and inspiring arrangements to encourage reading each month. From what Micah had shared a while ago, his girlfriend especially went all out during December, and he definitely wasn't lying.

Somehow, she'd created a cave-like living room with a huge comfy red armchair to the side. In it, sat the Grinch—life-size and in all his green and furry glory. He wore a bright red Santa suit, the hat tilted slightly over one eye. Strings of colored lights were haphazardly attached to the stone-like wall as a cut out window revealed snow and a peek of the moon.

It was hard to fully describe the level of awesome which was why I was glad we were required to take a selfie in front of it. This would be a photo I'd look at again and again.

"Holy shit!" Natalie exclaimed as she stepped closer to the window, her finger pressed against the glass. "She's even included a small Cindy Lou Who there on the floor with Max resting his head on her lap. She's reading to him from a Dr. Seuss book!"

Both our phones were out in a flash. I didn't care what people might have thought. Something told me part of the joy Sedona felt in being this creative was hearing how much others enjoyed it.

Somewhere in the back of my mind, I wondered if Eryx had seen this yet. We'd kind of left things hanging at the end of the semester—unsure exactly where we stood with each other after the incredible kiss we'd shared.

That kiss.

My toes *still* curled just thinking about it.

I wanted to be patient and not march up to his dorm room in Modi Tower and kick it down. I wanted to give into my dramatic tendencies and demand that he either tell me why he still acted all hesitant even after I declared—rather bravely—that I liked him a lot and wanted to be with him.

Luckily for him, the end of the semester brought finals and that conversation got lost amidst the hustle and bustle of making sure we all passed. Add the fact we'd all survived an insane semester of stress and danger made students a little giddy.

Time was running out for him, though. One of my New Year's resolutions was to go after what I wanted and not give up—even if it meant I had to lock myself in a room with him so he couldn't avoid me.

Anywho. It was tempting not to send him the photos I'd just taken. Maybe I would. Later. From one friend to another.

Maybe.

"Let's take the selfie so we can move on to the next clue," Natalie interrupted my thoughts. Her face was all flushed from the cold, but there was no mistaking she was having a good time. I was glad she hadn't cancelled and decided to stay home instead.

Huddled with our arms around each other, I stuck my phone out in front of us. "Say Christmas!" Making sure to get the display behind us and that we both looked cute, I took the photo. "Okay, one more but goofier."

Natalie stuck her tongue out to the side while I crossed my eyes and slanted my head toward her. Perfect.

After showing her, I tucked the phone back into my coat pocket and put my gloves back on. "Okay, next hint."

Straightening the paper, Natalie cleared her throat.

Next it will be a skip, hop, and jump,
To a place that is bustling with magic.
Their delicious elixirs and yummy baked treats,
Have turned days away from the tragic.

Go on inside and look for the guy,
With candy for buttons and ginger sweet.
Resist the urge to nibble on him,
But grab a hot drink—Micah's treat!

"It's like they already knew!" I whispered with a soft chuckle. The answer was a no-brainer. We'd already discussed stopping in at Coffee Haven to grab something warm before tackling the next part of the hunt but they'd already closed for the day. With Broastful Brew the only other coffee shop in town, that was our next destination, which was just fine with me. I adored both places because they fed my java addiction perfectly.

Natalie threaded her arm through mine. "Well, duh! How many times has Mr. Westbrook seen you without an insulated coffee cup in your hand since meeting you?" She bumped shoulders with me. "Come to think of it, for a while I thought it was your favorite accessory."

I ignored her teasing as I took in that first glorious inhale of the coffee shop. I loved everything about Broastful Brew—from the way a bell tinkled each time the door opened and closed, to the happy sounds of espresso machines being put through their paces, and how it could be a nice break from Coffee Haven's more electric energy and crowded atmosphere.

We quickly got in line and after a few moments placed our order with the barista. When she stood there waiting, I glanced at Natalie wondering if we'd missed something. The girl laughed and offered a goofy grin. "Micah Westbrook came in earlier and left money but told me you couldn't have your drinks until you added something to your order."

Ah, the trinket we were meant to gather.

We spoke up in unison. "We'd like a gingerbread man, thanks."

As she grabbed the tongs to slide the cookie into a paper bag, Natalie interrupted her—holding up two fingers. "Make that double."

I snorted. "Are you seriously telling me that you can eat an entire one right now?" I winced as I acknowledged how painfully tight my jeans still felt. "I'm full just breathing in here. In fact, I'm one sigh away from having the food sweats!"

Sometimes I wondered if my roomie simply tolerated my craziness and theatrics.

"Whatever, diva." She rolled her eyes at me and then handed me my drink. Magic was definitely in the air because we were in and out so quickly. "Let's go."

If the scavenger hunt continued to be this easy, we'd be back at Sedona and Micah's in no time.

This trinket can be found everywhere,
And makes the task complete.
It's also a sign to follow,
And the perfect place to meet.

Where big or small, bright or dimmed,
It brings together our small town.

So, if you've lost your Christmas spirit,
Just look up and lose your frown.

"I've got it!" I exclaimed and took a celebratory sip from my latte. At this rate, we were never leaving the town's square because everything we needed on the hunt was here. Micah, Sedona, and Holly had tried to be tricky with this clue, but they'd underestimated how competitive Natalie and I were. "What's the one place in town a visitor could tell what holiday season it was?"

"You mean other than all the white stuff that's been shoveled into piles?" Natalie wasn't wrong. Havenwood Falls received an obscene amount of snow already, and the forecasts all stated there was more to come.

We carefully crossed the street to the town square park, making sure not to slip on the patches of black ice. After almost breaking my neck and barely saving myself by grabbing hold of Natalie's arm, we finally reached the fountain. Standing in the center of the pretty square, we did exactly what the clue told us. We looked up, and wide smiles spread across our chilled cheeks.

"Havenwood Falls Christmas tree."

I nodded. "Yep, and in particular the beautiful crystal star at the top."

The twinkling that seemed to catch every flicker from neighboring lights was also fueled by magic. As a witch, I could sense the enchantment—unbeknownst to the humans milling about.

Natalie studied the paper. "It doesn't tell us whether we need to take a photo of it."

Leaning over her shoulder, I didn't see anything either. All it said was for us to look up.

"Hey, guys!" A cheerful voice came from behind. It was Addie Beaumont, one of the town's residents and the witch who registered each of its supernatural citizens and visitors. In fact, I wouldn't be surprised if Addie was responsible for the star's extra sparkle. "Sedona said you'd be here and asked me to give you this." Then without another word, she waved and left us holding a fabric wrapped gift.

Neither of us said a word until finally I caved. "Should we be scared?"

With gentle fingers, Natalie slowly pulled back the navy-blue material that was threaded with fine silver strands. Protected inside was a mini version of the town's star—twinkle and all.

"Scared of dropping it? Hell, yes," she answered in hushed tones. "Have you ever seen anything so perfect?"

I hadn't, and suddenly I was terrified of breaking it. "How are we going to carry this? In fact—" I paused for a second and raised the paper bag of gingerbread men. "How are we going to get all the trinkets back safely?"

A knowing grin was Natalie's answer. "You're not the only one with skills, Temp." She not only slipped the star into her shoulder bag, but also dropped the cookies in there as well. Neither of them should've fit.

"You *Hermione'd* your bag!" We both adored the Harry Potter books.

She nodded before picking her drink up again. Her brow wrinkled as she studied it. A few steps later, and the hot chocolate was abandoned in a nearby trash bin. "I did it to all my bags last semester so I could fit more things in them."

Ahh, a 'bigger on the inside' spell. She confirmed it by opening the bag and letting me peek inside.

I was impressed by her quick thinking.

"I love when your inner geek's showing. We make quite a team!" And with a happy high-five, we focused back on the list of hints.

We were almost half way through and confident we'd kick ass with the rest.

I knew our luck would run out and that not all the clues were surrounding the town square. Sooner or later, we'd need to cut through some of the streets to continue discovering the magic of Havenwood Falls.

The farther away we walked from the hustle and bustle that always seemed to fill the center of our new home, the quieter things grew between us. Maybe Natalie was mulling over the next clue. Or maybe, like me, she was caught up in memories.

"It should be around the corner." There was a tremor in her voice.

These beings sing from on high,
Of peace and hope from above.
You'll find your trinket in a place,
That holds memories of those we love.

Inside the steel-forged gates
Walk amongst both stones and earth,
This clue involves the resting place
For those embracing the opposite of birth.

We'd determined that our next clue had something to do with angels, but neither of us wanted to mention out loud exactly where we were going. Me, because I was mindful of my best friend's grief, and Natalie . . . well, I wouldn't blame her if she wanted to forget this clue and make up some excuse.

Stopping in front of a house with dimmed lights shining from within, I blew on my hands to warm them.

"Nat, I can go get the trinket for us," I offered, wanting to spare her the painful reminder of what she'd recently loss. "No one will think any less of you. I promise."

Natalie dusted off the snow that had fallen on the brick fence and leaned against it. She removed the now heavily creased paper from her bag, and after a second thought, also pulled out her phone.

"Just in case something happens," she added, snapping a photo of the list. She was prolonging the conversation.

Her bottom lip trembled, and her hands shook.

"Seriously. Let me do this." I wrapped my arms around her shoulders and pulled her close. "It's too soon."

Her mother had died, and although she liked to put on a brave face and show everyone that her world hadn't been forever changed, I knew better. I hated how helpless I felt—in not being able to soften the blow. All I could do was little things—listening, giving her space, small considerations. Anything to let her know she wasn't alone.

"I'm not fragile, Temp," she finally replied. Wiping her nose with the back of her hand, Natalie peered over at me. "Yes, my heart's broken, but I can't avoid life forever. Besides . . ." She stared off into the distance, pausing mid-thought. "I needed this . . . the scavenger hunt. I needed the reminder that I can't close off from the good just because I'm hurting."

My friend continuously amazed me with how she viewed her world. I could only hope I had the same grace and perspective when facing something similar.

"You sure?" The question came out before I could stop it. I already knew her answer.

"Yep." Pushing away from the fence, Natalie held out her hand. "Come on, let's keep going. I don't know about you, but my butt is cold now from sitting."

I was tempted to wave my hand and heat the air around us, courtesy of my growing fire magic, but Micah's warning rang through my mind again. While we were free to do spellwork back at campus, here in Havenwood Falls was a huge no-no.

"This would be so much warmer if I could use my powers," I grumbled beneath my breath.

"But where would the fun be in that!" Natalie chimed, unusually perky for someone close to being turned into an icicle. "It's all about the experience, Temp. Now hurry up!"

On our way again, Natalie's laugh sounded like music to my ears. "Yep, definitely worth keeping you around, Temp. You're like my own personal heater."

We returned to comfortable silence, and thankfully once we entered the cemetery grounds, it wasn't too hard finding our treasure. A small angel statue sat in the center of a nearby bench, all but glowing in a soft white light. The magic was courtesy of Sedona, and I wasn't going to lie—I was glad we didn't have to trek through the graves and stones to find it.

Judging by the sigh of relief Natalie let out, she was thinking the same thing.

Into her bag the angel went.

"I'm surprised they didn't use a Nativity scene or some kind of display like that for the clue." I'd been pondering that and couldn't figure it out. "Why have us come here?"

There was something peaceful about being here, surrounded by the dead, that I couldn't quite describe. Maybe it was because I was a witch and understood that life continued beyond death, but I didn't feel that same spooky feeling that my old friends had. Perhaps not giving credence to silly superstitions factored in. All I knew was a gentle energy pressed against me like a reassuring hug, and without thinking, I extended that to Natalie.

She returned my gesture. "Thank you." Her words were barely above a whisper. "I guess I needed that more than I realized."

Before I could come back with some sappy sentiment about there being more hugs where that came from, movement in my peripheral vision drew my attention.

Was that a light floating in the air?

"What the—?" I began, only to be interrupted by Natalie's own exclamation.

"Are you seeing this?" Moving away, her footsteps crunching on the snow beneath her boots, she peered into the growing shadows. "Is that . . . ?" A few more steps and she whipped around. "Tempest . . ."

I didn't need her to continue.

I recognized the owner of the glowing orb that hung suspended in the air.

Professor Phineas Knox.

He was here and following close behind him was the one guy who haunted my thoughts.

The one I dreamed of kissing again.

Eryx Strathos.

** *Continue Reading in FINDING THE MAGIC* **

Read about Tempest and Natalie in *Sun & Moon Academy Book One: Fall Semester* and *Sun & Moon Academy Book Two: Spring Semester*.

FINDING THE MAGIC

BY BELINDA BORING

An Eryx & Tempest Short Story

If someone had told me that I'd be traipsing through a cemetery on Christmas Eve, I'd have laughed at them. Yet here I was, walking behind one of my professors on a secret Santa mission.

Campus was pretty much a ghost town at the moment, and while I enjoyed the solitude, even I was going a little stir-crazy over being alone. That's why I'd practically jumped at Professor Knox's invitation to join him tonight—agreeing before he'd even had a chance to explain what his plans were exactly.

And here we were. Weaving between gravestones with spelled bags filled with gifts. What an unlikely pair we were—Secret Santas minus the red suits, bellies like a bowl of jelly, and white beards.

"You do know that the dead can't accept gifts, right?" I whispered, mindful for some reason that I didn't disturb the peace and quiet that filled the air. Even the crunching of snow beneath my boots sounded comforting.

While I hadn't taken an Alchemy class, I knew that when it was time, Professor Knox would become one of my favorites. He had a friendly demeanor that made it easy to talk with him, and in the few hours we'd been together, we'd discussed a wide variety of topics. Right now, we were between subjects. Neither of us were forthcoming about our past and what brought us to Havenwood Falls.

I liked that he didn't pry.

"That doesn't mean they should be forgotten," Knox replied over his shoulder. "If there's one thing I've learned from Marcus is that memories should be cherished and held on to. These children are still beloved and important."

Marcus. Marcus St. James. Now he was someone I would love to know about. I briefly met him when Knox stopped by his home for last minute details. If I understood their brief conversation, the idea of a local Secret Santa originated from the reclusive vampire and was a tradition they both continued throughout the years.

I didn't quite understand the dynamics between the two men, but if I were to wager a guess, I'd say they were family just in the way they moved about. I'd gotten really good at reading people's body language over the years. It was a vital skill that had saved my ass more times than I can count.

Even though he couldn't see, I nodded. "Okay, so we're to leave the small hearts on each headstone?"

With gloved hands, I brushed my thumb over the crystal ornament that twinkled when a facet caught a stray beam of light. The hearts were exquisite—beautifully crafted—a labor of love by Marcus who had fashioned them with his own two hands.

"That's the plan." Knox was already reverently placing them, his mouth moving silently as though leaving a small blessing with the hearts.

We worked side by side, row by row, until finally each of the ornaments had been given. I wondered what family members would say when they next came to pay their respects and found the small gift. Would they take it home and place it on their trees as a forever keepsake?

Snowflakes swirled and danced in the air, spreading nature's own version of Christmas magic. I blew warm breath into my cupped hands, and stomped my feet, hoping that would chase away the coldness around us. Damn, it was beyond chilly.

"So what's next?" I asked, waiting for directions to our next stop. We were working under the cloak of darkness, trying to make sure no one spotted us, which wasn't always easy. I swear Havenwood Falls always had someone up and about—despite the weather or time.

Knox pulled out a piece of paper, even though I was pretty sure he had it memorized. "Whisper Falls Inn. Madame Luiza is expecting us by the back door. If we hurry, she'll have some hot chocolate waiting." There was a huge grin on his face. "Trust me, it's the best you'll ever taste." He was practically smacking his lips together.

I didn't bother telling him I'd lived long enough to have heard that declaration from all around the world. Everyone thought theirs was the best.

"So," he continued, after slinging his bag over his shoulder. "What do you think of your first semester at SMA?" We'd ended up in the center of the cemetery and were now headed in the direction of the exit. At least Knox knew where he was going.

My gaze darted back and forth—more out of habit—knowing full well that I wouldn't be able to see clearly in the dark. While I didn't sense any danger, I knew I couldn't completely let my guard down. Havenwood Falls had proven safe so far, but that could change in the blink of an eye. I'd seen that happen too many times to fully believe in my safety.

Oh, the joys of being hunted by a Goddess.

Did I tell Knox that this wasn't the first time I'd attended a college or university? When centuries lay before you, education was a suitable way to pass the time.

"I love it," I admitted. I spoke the truth. Being amongst others who held magic and shared similar gifts made life a little more interesting. "Although, who knew attending could be so . . ." I searched for the right word to describe the insanity that happened. The image of an hourglass surfaced in my mind. "Brutal."

And, for the hundredth time today, my mind changed tracks. No matter what I was doing, or my failed attempts to control my thoughts, I instantly saw a face.

Her face.

Tempest Bell.

She haunted me—those kisses that should've been impossible. Her presence confused the hell out of me, and despite the overwhelming pull I felt toward her, fear kept her at arm's distance.

I'm sure I pissed her off.

If her being mad at me kept her safe from my curse—from who I am—then I would be the asshole. Even if it killed me a little each time.

Knox let out a low whistle. "I think brutal is the right word, Eryx. I've seen a lot in my lifetime, and the way you students were tested was absolutely insane. Here's hoping next semester is less chaotic and more academic." He slowed so we could walk side by side. "Are you taking my class?"

Professor Knox taught alchemy, a fascinating subject I knew little about.

I shrugged. "I haven't finalized my schedule yet, but if I can, I will."

He grunted in agreement. "Don't think I'll go easy on you, if you do. I can't show I have favorites."

His comment caught me by surprise. "Aww, you like me. I'm flattered."

Knox pulled off his hat and shook out his blond hair. "Don't go making this awkward, Strathos." He chuckled as he shoved the beanie into his pocket. "You could say I'm always hardest on those I like better. You may come to wish that I hated you."

I blew out a *hmph*. "Bring it."

Our easygoing banter was cut short by the sound of nearby voices. So far we'd been alone, and thankfully we were done with this portion of our mission. Secret Santa was still just that—a secret.

"Hey," Knox said, his gaze straining to make out the two figures up ahead. "Don't you know those two?"

My heart thudded. I didn't know many people in town, and for the most part, the other students were off visiting family or keeping to themselves on campus. The last place I expected to meet anyone was here at the cemetery—especially on Christmas Eve.

The closer we got, the more I recognized them.

Shit. One of them was someone I most wanted to see, and in the same breath, the last person I wanted to bump into.

Tempest Bell.

For some reason, she was here with her best friend and roommate Natalie Putnam.

"Maybe we should hide," I volunteered, already stepping backward. It was a cowardly move, but I didn't care.

Knox looked at me like I'd suddenly grown two heads or something. "You want to hide from them?" When I didn't answer, he laughed. "Well, that's interesting. We come across two beautiful young women, and you'd rather retreat than go say hello. I was thinking we could see if they wanted to help. The more the merrier."

I wanted to curl up into a tight ball and disappear. Hell, I'd have settled for those hunting for me to show up—locking me into a battle of life or death. Anything to avoid seeing Tempest and having to resist those gorgeous brown eyes. It killed me not to take her in my arms.

"We have history," I confessed. "They're from the Academy, and I've been a jerk to one of them." I didn't get to explain further, despite the look of curiosity that now filled Professor Knox's face. "I'm pretty sure they'd rather be anywhere on the planet than here."

Ugh, I needed to shut the hell up before I totally looked like an idiot. I already sounded like one.

It was too late to hide anyway. They'd seen us. I knew because Tempest's step faltered the second she recognized who was approaching them—the way her smile changed when she saw who was with Professor Knox.

This is what you want, idiot, I silently chided myself. *You want to keep her away.*

Oh, what a magnificent lie that was.

❊

It was as if I was invisible because Tempest looked everywhere *but* where I was standing. I deserved it.

"You're more than welcome to join us," Knox said, including me in the invitation. "We've got a few more places to stop by, and I can't speak for Eryx here, but I'm ready to get out of the cold." He elbowed me as though he could jostle me into talking.

"Uh, yeah," was all I could say. I was definitely an idiot.

Humor filled Knox's eyes, and a knowing look passed between him and Natalie. What that meant exactly was anyone's guess, but it didn't take long for the truth to surface.

"Well, we're on a scavenger hunt," Natalie shared, her voice bubbly with excitement. She waved a creased piece of paper in the air, and I briefly caught a glimpse of the words. "Sedona and Micah," she caught herself for a second. "I mean, Professor Westbrook created it with his daughter, Holly, for us to . . ." Her eyes fell to the writing, and she recited what was written there. "To discover the magic of Havenwood Falls."

It wasn't hard to believe that these two were loved by the town's couple.

Knox beamed as he listened. "Don't trip yourself over formalities, Natalie. We're not on campus right now so we're all simply friends." He leaned in to have a look at the paper. "I don't think we can compete with this, Eryx. While playing Secret Santa is a form of magic itself, theirs looks like a lot of fun."

Why did I feel elated in one breath that this awkward moment was about to end and then devastated that it also meant I'd be watching Tempest leave? I swear these emotions were giving me whiplash and driving me crazy.

"What a shame," I muttered, sounding more and more like a fool.

Later I would ask myself whether or not I wanted to thank Natalie or dig myself a hole in the ground to hide in.

"Why can't we do both?" With a quick glance at her quiet friend,

Natalie began to compare notes with Professor Knox. "I'm pretty sure if we team up, we can kill two birds with one stone, so to speak." Dragging Tempest over to where she stood, the three of them were soon nodding. "Then it's decided!"

Natalie had her phone out, her thumbs moving back and forth over the screen. "There, Temp," she announced, returning the device back to her pocket. "I just sent you the photo of the list. You go to this one and this one, and we'll meet back at the town square once we're finished."

It was clear that I'd have no say in the matter.

Tempest was now staring at her best friend. "Are you sure? I thought we were going to do this together."

It was obvious she wasn't happy with the change of plans. The realization bruised my ego.

Giving her a hug, Natalie whispered into Tempest's ear, before they both turned around to look at me. Tempest shook her head. Natalie answered with a reassuring smile.

"This also gives me a chance to talk to Professor Knox about his class before next semester. Alchemy is such an interesting subject." Natalie all but pushed her friend toward me. "Take good care of my bestie, Strathos. You don't want to mess with a pissed off witch."

I didn't want to mess with a pissed off Tempest, either, but it seemed like I wasn't given much of a choice.

"I'll keep her safe," I promised, already scrambling to think of something to say that would make the next few hours less uncomfortable. This all happened because of that damn kiss. That one incredible kiss. The most tragic kiss in existence.

"Let's go then," Tempest uttered, pushing past me. She wasn't happy. I'd ruined her plans and evening. I was definitely the jerk she'd accused me of.

I gave one last pleading look to Professor Knox, watching as he left with Natalie.

I was the killer of Christmas magic.

Great.

❄

"Did you need any help with the clues?" I asked, after what felt like an agonizingly long time walking in silence. "I'm pretty good at figuring things out." It wasn't a brag either. I grew up having to solve riddles and searching for loopholes.

For a second, I thought Tempest hadn't heard me, or if she had, that she was planning on ignoring me. Despite having been pushed together, if being with me was truly that awful, I would walk her to wherever she needed to go and say goodnight. I wasn't that desperate to be with her that I'd do it under coercion.

"You don't have to worry about it," came her soft response.

This was horrible. The Tempest I knew was feisty and in-your-face. She spoke her mind and had no problem telling me how she felt. Whoever it was walking beside me barely said a peep. I had to fix this.

"Look," I started, slowing down so I could gently grab her arm. She didn't flinch or pull away so that was something. "I don't want you to hate me, Tempest. I meant it when I said I wanted us to be friends."

After the euphoria of being able to safely kiss her that one night had passed, common sense kicked in with a brutal vengeance. I couldn't risk that my curse would come flaring back into life—snatching away the small piece of happiness I'd found with Tempest. It had killed me to place us back in the friend-zone again. What destroyed me most, however, was the way I saw my words breaking her heart. She'd valiantly tried to brush my decision off, acting as if it didn't matter to her at all. The problem was it *did* mean something to me.

We'd spent the final weeks of classes walking on eggshells around each other—the chemistry between us never really fading. If anything, I wanted her more now than ever.

I bent my knees a little so I could capture her gaze. Part of me wished I hadn't, because what I found there was nothing like the quiet field mouse façade she'd been projecting.

She was pissed.

If looks could kill, she'd have set me on fire.

Fire . . . I could deal with that.

"You don't want to have this conversation right now, Eryx." She all but hissed at me through her teeth. "Please. Let's just get through tonight and try to salvage what little Christmas spirit we can."

Sometimes I'm stupidly stubborn.

Like right this instant.

"I do want this conversation, Tempest. I'm not going to spend the next few hours with someone who hates my guts. If you'd rather be somewhere else—" I hated how I sounded. "With someone else, then speak up, and I'll take you there."

Her eyes widened, and I swear, I saw her magic crackle and spark. Shit.

"I don't need you taking me anywhere, Eryx Strathos. I don't need your permission, and I sure as hell don't need you acting like you're the victim in all this."

Say what?

This girl was twisting me up in knots, and not the good kind. "That's not what I meant. I was just trying to be a nice guy."

Judging by the loud snort, my comment amused her. "Don't you think it's too late for that?" There were tears forming in her eyes, and the second she realized I saw, Tempest angrily wiped them away. "Ugh, Eryx."

I considered myself lucky that she wasn't throwing hexes at me.

I knew what the issue was—the emotional elephant that sat between us whenever we were together. I just didn't know how I could make her understand without telling her every sordid detail from my past. The risk with that was once she knew, would she still want anything to do with me?

These were all too heavy for Christmas Eve contemplations.

Shaking the thoughts loose, I did the next best thing. "How about this?" I took both her hands in mine and squeezed them lightly, hoping with all my heart that she'd sense my sincerity. "Once Christmas is over, I'll answer every question you have. No more evading. If you want the truth, I'll deliver it on a silver platter."

Waiting for her response was as paralyzing as my curse. All I knew was that I couldn't go on like this with her—especially her. If there was ever someone I could bare my soul to, my heart whispered it might be Tempest Bell.

"Are you lying, Eryx? Because I don't think I could forgive you if you were." The doubt that filled her voice was my fault.

"I give you my word."

Tempest slipped her hands out of mine and held up her pinky. "Has anyone ever told you how dangerous it is to break a witch's pinky promise?"

I shook it without hesitation. "Cross my heart. Hope to die."

That made her laugh, and it was like freaking music to my ears. "Shit, slow down, Strathos. I believe you." She reached into her pocket and pulled out her phone. "I guess you should look at the clues Natalie left for me. Convince me you're worth keeping around."

She was back to being the teasing Tempest I knew. By some miracle, the tension between us began to diffuse.

And in my mind, I fist bumped the air.

Knox hadn't been stretching the truth. The hot chocolate here at Whisper Falls Inn was definitely superior—each mouthful deliciously decadent. What he hadn't added was that this drink would ruin me for all others. Now that I'd tasted Madame Luiza's famous recipe, prepared by inn's kitchen staff, I suspected I'd be comparing it to everything else.

"What do you think?" I asked.

Tempest held the cup up to her lips and gently blew across the steaming surface. "Is it bad that I want to take a bath in this stuff?" With her eyes closed, I was free to study her enjoyment. God, she was beautiful. "I'm pretty sure Coffee Haven doesn't compete with this. Just wow."

When her lids popped open and she caught me watching her, Tempest smiled.

My heart instantly melted.

"I did warn you!" an older voice came from behind us as we sat on the porch steps at the back of the inn. We'd already delivered the presents for the kids staying over the holiday season, with a few extras to give away at the inn's discretion, I scooted closer to Tempest as our new friend descended the steps.

Did I mention we were talking to a ghost? Knox hadn't bothered to include that important piece of information when he hurriedly told me where to take this batch of Christmas gifts. Only that with a busy night ahead, we might have trouble finding someone.

We'd found Madame Luiza almost instantly.

"Can I interest you in a baked treat before you leave?"

Something told me that she wouldn't accept any form of refusal.

"Are they in the kitchen as well?" I asked, already standing. If the cookies were anything like the hot chocolate, I needed to taste them.

The ghostly figure nodded, and I raced inside, catching a glimpse of one of the employees on my return. The teen girl simply glared at me, her eyes darting up and down like she was trying to assess whether I posed a threat.

"Happy holidays!" I called out, eager to get back to Tempest. Like an idiot, I waved the two treats I held for her to see. "Thank you."

I didn't wait for a response, and finally back outside, I handed over one of the cookies.

"So," Tempest began, talking around her first bite. "Are you looking for any part-time employees? You can just pay me in cookies." She giggled when her next bite crumbled between her lips.

Oh, to be a crumb.

Shit, my thoughts weren't helping at all.

"Maybe I'll take one for the road as well," I mumbled, hoping that my face wasn't as red as it felt. "Rub it in to Professor Knox that he missed out."

"Oh, you silly boy. He's already stopped by and introduced young Natalie Putnam to me. What a delightful girl." Madame Luiza winked at Tempest. "I can see you two causing a lot of mischief up there at the Academy."

"We do our best." Tempest stood and stepped closer to the kind woman, as though wanting to hug her but realized she couldn't. There was something comforting about Madame Luiza—the way she made you instantly feel like you were part of her family.

I almost choked on my cookie when she interrupted my thoughts. "It's because Havenwood Falls *is* about family. That's part of the magic."

Tempest dropped the paper napkin she was holding as she fumbled for her phone. "Crap, that reminds me! I'm meant to be doing a scavenger hunt right now and looking for clues. I actually think this one might be about you . . . well, about the inn."

> *This trinket will warm you.*
> *and not just for ice cold feet.*
> *In the spirit of family,*
> *Of love, and hot treats.*

> *If looking for magic,*
> *You couldn't go wrong.*
> *Find where happiness whispers,*
> *A soft Christmas song.*

"Short and sweet," I murmured, staring down at the screen.

Tempest nodded as she took another bite of the iced sugar cookie. "Just like this . . ." She immediately looked up to find Madame Luiza grinning like the Cheshire cat from Alice in Wonderland. "Does this mean you have a trinket for me?"

The older lady gestured to the railing, and for the first time, I saw a small paper gift bag. "Micah was very strict on the rules. I had to wait until you asked me about it and not blurt out the secret and ruin the surprise." That last part seemed to irk her. "I keep many secrets, mind you. I know how to play this game."

Waiting until Tempest held the surprise in her hands—a small bundle that was rolled up tightly with a red and silver glitter ribbon—she asked, "Can you guess what it is without unravelling it?"

When Tempest cocked her head, the dark brown strands of her hair fell across her face, and it took every ounce of willpower I had not to capture them with my fingers. Every time the night's breeze caught Tempest just right, I was hit with the fruity scent of her shampoo and the subtle fragrance of her perfume. Everything about this woman was intoxicating, and it was in this precise moment, I knew I was losing the fight with my self-imposed control.

"Hmmm," she said, turning the item about in her hand, her thumb rubbing softly over the knitted fabric. "Considering all the other clues were Christmas themed, I'm going to say . . . that this . . . is . . . stockings?"

Madame Luiza clapped her hands under her chin. "Yes! I believe there's one there for both you and your roommate."

She positively radiated with maternal pride.

Tempest held them up to her chest. "Then we will cherish them forever. Thank you so much. You've been more than generous."

They hugged each other awkwardly—Madame Luiza couldn't really touch Tempest—leaving me standing at the side. Not that I minded. I was just happy to be there.

She held her hands around the sides of Tempest's face. "Merry Yuletide, child. May the Goddess watch over you always and guide your steps." She cast a quick glance toward me. "And watch out for this one. He wears his heart on his sleeve for you. Be gentle."

Before another word could be said, Madame Luiza hurried us on our way. As I turned, I felt a smack on my ass that made me jump and heard a ghostly giggle drift away. Tempest and I both laughed.

According to my list, we were done with the Secret Santa deliveries —and that brought me closer to saying goodnight to my current partner-in-crime.

"Soo," I drawled, not sure how to start up a conversation after that last piece of advice. If only Madame Luiza knew that I was the one who needed to be gentle—that I'd been the one to crash and tumble all over Tempest's heart. "How did you enjoy being Secret Santa? Is it what you expected?"

Damn, I wish I could read her mind, instead of relying on body language.

"It's been fun," she answered cautiously. "This wasn't how I expected to spend the evening, but I've always wanted to be part of something like this. Maybe—" She bit her bottom lip and the image played over and over in my mind. "Professor Knox will let Natalie and I be a part of it next year. Maybe we'll even get to meet the mysterious Marcus St. James."

I was relieved to hear her say that. Not the Marcus part, but that I hadn't ruined her night. "I caught a brief glimpse of him earlier, and Knox mentioned that his friend prefers doing things behind the scenes."

She nodded, looking both ways before we walked across the small lane, walking aimlessly in a quiet part of town. The snow had stopped falling, and it was just me and her . . . and a million stars twinkling above us in the sky. "Then this is definitely a great job for him. Only a few people know what's happening. I like that."

"Yeah?"

Tempest kicked some of the snow that had been pushed to the edge of the sidewalk we were on. "Where I'm from, no good deed was done anonymously. My parents loved to make a big fuss over all their charity giving. It became pretty obvious that they were only in it for the praise of being seen. Not like this. This is doing good because it comes from the heart." She glanced over at me. "Know what I mean?"

I did. I knew exactly the same sentiment. "It becomes about look at me . . . worship me . . . see how generous I am." There was a particular goddess who came to mind, but I didn't utter her name. As safe as I felt in Havenwood Falls, I didn't dare tempt the Fates.

"I don't want to be part of that anymore. I didn't like how empty it made me feel. That's not how you find love and earn respect." There was something wistful in her tone that told me she'd thought a lot about it.

"If it matters in the slightest, I don't think you have to worry about that. You don't come across as shallow." My response made her burst out into laughter. "What? Did I say something wrong?"

Tempest covered her mouth in a vain attempt to suppress her amusement. "No. You just caught me by surprise. I've been called shallow and prissy and spoiled most of my life. It's nice to hear someone doesn't think so poorly of me." All I wanted to tell her was those people were idiots, but when she gently shook her head, I kept quiet. "Thank you. For what it's worth, your opinion means a lot."

We walked on in silence, but this time there was nothing oppressive or awkward about it. I felt like we were truly two friends out on a mission which was definitely progress.

If she'd have asked me right there and then—cheesy or not—I'd have declared I'd discovered the magic because I felt hope between us. That maybe, just maybe, things would work out.

Not every story had to end as a tragedy, right?

My phone buzzed, and it was Knox letting me know that he'd finished all the deliveries and helped Natalie gather up the next to last scavenger hunt item from Fallview Tavern. All that was left was one, and Tempest's roommate wanted her to come back to the town's square to complete it together.

Our night was coming to a close, and I was nowhere near ready for it.

From the sound of Tempest's voice, she was disappointed too—or maybe that was more wishful thinking on my part.

As we walked, she read out loud the final hint.

"I think we're overthinking this," Tempest said, her brow furrowed in concentration. "What's the saying? When faced with a problem that stumps you, just kiss."

Oh God, did she really just say that? My heart thundered in

anticipation, betraying my need to keep her in the friend zone. "You want us to what?"

Her lips moved slowly as she silently reread the hint.

"What?" I could see the exact moment when she realized what she'd said—her face draining of all color. Even white as a sheet she looked beautiful. "No!" she blurted out forcefully. Her cheeks were now a blazoned red. "It's something Natalie likes to tell me. KISS—meaning keep it simple, silly." Her finger traced over the words again, her woolen gloves scratching softly over the paper. "See. This. I think this is relevant." She pointed to the words *beneath* and then *kiss*.

My eyes skimmed the verses.

This trinket showed up a long time ago,
Often linked with fertility and peace.
It's not just found at Christmas,
But as far back as Ancient Greece.

War generals kissed beneath it,
Celts and druids used it to heal the sick.
And if you find yourself under it,
Then you better act real quick!

"Ten bucks says Sedona wrote this. She loves random facts like this," Tempest murmured.

I'd stopped reading along with Tempest, and instead openly studied her. "I didn't know that about the generals. The more you know, right?"

It was only when she looked up at me that I darted my eyes away.

"Knowledge is always good," I murmured. The only good thing about mistletoe was it gave you an excuse to kiss. My gaze dropped to Tempest's mouth, and the longing I felt was like a sucker-punch to the gut. I was torturing myself. I should've spoken up and partnered with Natalie instead, but the thought of Knox with Tempest soured my stomach. I craved this brunette with everything inside me. It was the closest I'd felt to being an addict—knowing how badly each second in her presence burned me . . . changed me . . . yet not caring enough to walk away.

Tempest searched the area. "So the problem isn't that we didn't figure the clue out, but that we don't know where to start looking for it." She turned around in a slow circle. "Mistletoe could be anywhere."

She was right. "And we're sure it's mistletoe?"

She nodded. "Do you think they want us to go looking down one of the trails that lead out to the lake or mountains?" Reluctance had crept into her voice, and I didn't blame her. The last thing I wanted to do was go traipsing off where we'd get lost—maybe fall down a well where only Lassie could find us.

I knew it with a hundred percent surety. "No. Above all, they'd never compromise your safety. The mistletoe is nearby. We just need to think . . ." My words fell away as a single word surfaced in my mind.

Kiss.

Keep it simple, silly.

As the fragile thought began to form, I remembered something Knox and Marcus had mentioned earlier that night. Something was always going on in Havenwood Falls, and tonight wasn't any different. At the town square's gazebo, a large group would be gathered, and if we hurried, we'd get there in time to find the next trinket.

"I think you're right. We just need to kiss." I grabbed her hand and began to race toward the town's center, and the closer I got, the more details I was able to see. It wasn't just any party.

It was a wedding—the perfect place for a memorable kiss.

Together we approached, mindful not to interrupt, and sure enough . . . mingled with the decorations were sprigs of mistletoe.

"Do you think they'd mind if we stole one?" Tempest whispered, mirroring what I was already contemplating. Not waiting for an answer, she plucked one that was hanging and quickly stuffed it into her bag with a soft giggle. "Like Natalie likes to say, better to ask forgiveness than permission."

Our focus kept being tugged toward the couple exchanging marriage vows, which I guess was better than thinking about the mistletoe in Tempest's hand. I wanted to snatch it from her, hold it above her head, and lean in for a kiss. It was a horrible idea—especially after the way the evening went. If I wanted to undo all the magic that had softly been whispering between us, softening hurt feelings, then I'd do the guy thing and blunder on in without thinking.

Luckily, I didn't have to worry too hard because it was then that Knox and Natalie showed up, out of breath and rosy cheeked.

"Holy cow, it's freaking cold!" Natalie exclaimed. "Any colder and I could cut glass with my nipples!" Knox struggled to stifle his chuckle. Tempest cocked her brow and smirked. "Well, you know what I mean. Brrrr!"

"I'll take that as my cue to leave. Can you see the girls safely home, Eryx?" It was more of an order than a question. I shook Knox's extended hand, and he clasped my forearm. "Stop by the house before the next semester starts. Don't rattle around in that tower by yourself. Take it from me—solitude can change a man."

Wishing Natalie and Tempest a merry Yuletide, Knox took off across the street toward his home.

"So," Natalie said, glancing between us. "How was it? I'm trusting things went well considering the fact you're both standing here in one piece." It had been a risk on her part to push us together, and I could tell the way she studied her bestie that she wasn't quite convinced she'd made the right move.

Tempest wasn't going to let her friend off the hook. Even I grew impatient waiting for her response. "Well . . ." Natalie was ready to throttle her. "It was okay." She winked at me, and I chuckled, my warm breath forming small white clouds.

"So I worried for nothing, huh?" Natalie threaded her arms through both mine and Tempest's. "In fact, you can almost say I performed a Christmas miracle. Yay me!"

We both groaned at her—loudly.

"Where to next?" I asked. Tempest replied "Micah's" while Natalie chimed in "home."

"Pick one." I chuckled. "We can't be in two places at once."

Thankfully Natalie came up with the solution. "Sedona texted and said there was a change of plans. They heard about us helping with Secret Santa, and told us to go home afterward, that they'll catch up with us tomorrow when we come for dinner." She directed her next comment to me. "And seeing as you didn't make my bestie cry, they also invited you over for Christmas."

With the night drawing to a close, we headed back to the campus portal—tired but happy. Who would've thought that a simple trek through the cemetery would've resulted in this—one of the best Christmas Eves of my life?

Walking back through campus felt different now. Maybe what had been missing was the magic that Natalie and Tempest had gone searching for. Or maybe I just realized I didn't want to be alone on Christmas Eve—that for all my running and hiding, it felt good to press pause on all that drama and simply breathe.

As we approached the red doors of Hel Tower, I took that as my cue to excuse myself and leave the girls for the night. Nothing screamed awkward more than being the unwanted third wheel who couldn't take a hint and go home.

"Thanks for the evening, guys," I said, stopping before I climbed the stairs. "I'm glad we got to see each other and have some fun." I was already turning away when Natalie chimed in.

"Are you seriously going to ditch us after coming this far?" She retraced her steps and tugged on my arm. "In all honesty, you helped with the scavenger hunt, so you're obligated to see it through to the end."

I peered over her shoulder and up to where Tempest stood at the door. "Would that be okay?"

My heart raced, beating loud enough that it thundered in my ears. I felt like an idiot standing there, praying she'd say yes.

Instead she shrugged. "Well, it wouldn't be fair for us to exclude you now. You were my partner-in-crime after all."

And with her hip, Tempest shoved against the door and entered the building.

They didn't give me much time to look about, but their home was definitely different from my own. Modi Tower didn't have the same gothic feel Hel did—decorated in crystals and red and black furniture. It reminded me of some of the luxurious places I'd stayed in over the centuries. I couldn't wait to see what their room looked like.

With a dramatic flair, Tempest whipped about and used her arms to block me from following them into their room. "Before you're granted the extreme privilege of venturing where no other guy has gone before, repeat these words after me." She paused, lowering her voice. "I, Eryx Strathos."

I wiped all expression from my face and nodded. "I, Eryx Strathos."

"Vow a most solemn oath that the things I'm about to witness will never be uttered outside the confines of this room."

I repeated verbatim—almost failing to keep from smirking. Tempest thought she was being serious, when in fact, I found her utterly adorable.

"Should I break this contract, let it be known that I not only bring . . ."

I mirrored her words.

". . . dishonor on myself, dishonor on my family, but also . . ." Tempest peered closely at me—her face inches away from mine. "I hope you realize what you're getting yourself into, Eryx. Once uttered, you can't take it back."

The corner of my mouth lifted into a half-smile.

"But also?" I prompted. I could see Natalie from the corner of my eye, shaking from suppressed laughter. I felt a tickle start in my chest, and I knew, if I didn't finish whatever this was, I'd come dangerously close to chuckling in Tempest's face. "But also?" I said again.

She cleared her throat. "I'll bring dishonor on my family, and dishonor on my cow!"

Tempest completely broke her façade, and with her arms wrapped around her waist, bent over laughing.

Say what?

"Dishonor on my what?"

Natalie stepped forward and whipped her own arm out. "Whoa, are you telling me you've never heard that before?" She didn't hesitate to raise up on her tiptoes and lock eyes. "Maybe we shouldn't let you in our room!"

These two were crazy. "I know exactly where it came from. I'm not a complete heathen."

Tempest had finally found her composure and straightened up. "Fine. Where then?"

I tried to answer as humbly as I could. "Mulan. *Mushu* to be exact."

They looked at each other quickly, and then as one, stepped to the side. "Then you may enter. Remember your oath. Don't condemn your cow."

Rolling my eyes, I entered their room, and any sarcastic comment that had been dancing in my mind disappeared. What I saw was so pretty and magical. Based on their surprised gasps, Natalie and Tempest were amazed too.

"What the heck?" Tempest exclaimed, rushing forward to grab the large note that was attached to the beautifully decorated Christmas tree. Everywhere we looked, fairy lights twinkled from where someone had carefully hung them. "Did you know about this, Nat?"

Her roommate was already shaking her head, examining the seven-foot tree—the scent of pine filling the air. "Dude, I've been busy all night."

Their focus zeroed in on me, and I held my hands up in submission. "Not guilty, although I wish I had because this is seriously cool."

Standing side-by-side, they opened the folded note and silently mouthed what they were reading. Both of them sighed and ooohed, until Natalie finished and placed her hand over her heart. "They did this for us. This was part of the scavenger hunt."

Tempest handed me the letter, and sure enough, it was signed by Micah, Sedona, and Holly.

"They wanted to do something special for us, and look!" Tempest plucked one of the ornaments from the tree. "The decorations represent each of the trinkets."

The candy cane.

The gingerbread man.

The twinkling lights.

Some shiny baubles.

Glittery angels.

"Wait, we're missing a few things." Tempest reached into her bag and pulled out the stockings and mistletoe. "We're just missing lights. I wonder if they were forgotten?"

In the excitement of discovering what hung from the tree branches, they hadn't read the note to the end. Good thing I had.

"Guys, I promise you, they've thought of everything." Sure enough, at the very end, someone, Sedona presumably, had added a small incantation.

Holding hands, Natalie and Tempest recited the spell, and it was fascinating to watch the two witches wield magic. There was nothing overbearing about the energy that gently danced through the air—nothing like the power that I'd seen thrown my way. It was almost poetic in nature.

As they uttered one final blessed be, a beautiful light burst into life, stretching out to take the form of a long string of light orbs that the girls directed onto the tree. I wasn't too afraid to admit that it left me feeling a little speechless.

"Perfect," Tempest whispered.

Yes, standing there basking in the glow of the magic she'd helped create, a gentle smile lighting her up from within—yes, she was absolutely perfect.

"Merry Christmas, Tempest," I said as I joined her and Natalie. "Thanks for including me."

My gaze drifted over to the mistletoe still lying on her bed where she'd dropped it to work the spell.

There'd be plenty of time to claim that kiss beneath it.

Scratch that—a lifetime of mistletoe kisses—and she was worth the wait.

Read about Eryx and Tempest in *Sun & Moon Academy Book One: Fall Semester* and *Sun & Moon Academy Book Two: Spring Semester.*

SANTA'S LITTLE HELPERS

BY T.V. HAHN

A Teeny Weeny Short Story

This was Tang Wu's first winter holiday season in Havenwood Falls. He loved the Hot Cocoa and Cookie Crawl. I never saw anyone eat so many cookies and not gain a gram! But of course, that might be the magic of Havenwood Falls.

Mat, once again, found the most beautiful spruce and set it up in my townhome's parlor. The pixies completed their adornment of popcorn and cranberry garland, albeit typically a bit haphazard, and Cyllene, my long time dryad friend, did the honors of lighting each of the tiny candles at the end of every branch, with the twirl of her magnificent swallow-like tail.

It'd been a long night, this Christmas Eve, with the late wedding in the square finishing only moments ago. Now, the scent of pine mingled with the aroma of my freshly baked pumpkin spice cookies, wafting through the room as each of us settled cozily before the fireplace in our unassigned positions. That is, my extremely tall and muscular nephew Mat sat on the overstuffed chair, and his fiancée—another one of my closest friends—Nina, sat on his lap, both of them cuddling romantically under the fleece throw cover. I sat on the right end of the settee, my legs curled under me, comfortably watching

Tang's handsome face and listened as he began to read *A Visit From St. Nicholas* by Clement Moore, who by the way was a professor of Oriental and Greek Literature, not to mention divinity. Because of that, I thought Tang took a real liking to the story and the history. Certainly, Cyllene was enamored, either by Tang or the story, as she rested on Tang's shoulder as he so eloquently read the last line, ". . . and to All a Good Night."

Tang bowed his head at the end of the reading, as he slowly and methodically closed the book. Then, the scene of tranquility and peace changed rapidly, as the pixie sisters, who had been mesmerized by Tang's reading while sitting on the hearth, suddenly jumped up and began cheering and yapping something about being Santa's Helpers on the night before Christmas. All four of them—Tierri, Enya, Aeri, and Ushka—pranced and danced, yammered and yelled. At least until Ushka and Enya began wrestling on the hearth rug.

"STOP!" I commanded the pixie pranksters. Sometimes a shouted command was the only thing they would listen to. "I know the story you want to tell Tang, Nina, and Mat. But really, you all need to decide who is going tell it."

It was a good direction, sort of. Now the four imps began arguing, rabbit punching, and, once again, wrestling over who would tell the story. It didn't help that both Tang and Mat found them completely amusing. Alas, they all agreed that Tierri could start the tale, since she was the first one who was encountered by the extra-terrestrial also known as Santa Claus.

Enya, Aeri, and Ushka sat on the hearth, and Tierri stood front and center to tell the story.

"Once upon a Christmas," she began, and the three pixies on the hearth bobbing their heads up and down in agreement, "in a land far, far away!"

Aeri jumped up from her seat on the hearth. "Yeah, the Isle of Gwynf'l!"

"Shush!" Tierri admonished. "I'm telling this story! Be quiet, and sit down!"

Enya jumped up to defend her other sister. "Don't tell her to be quiet. She's right!"

Ushka sprang to her feet, too. "I was there!"

"Me too!" Aeri said.

"Me three!" Enya added.

"Yeah, yeah. Me four and one," Tierri said. "It was the night before Christmas on the Isle of Gwynf'l, and our elf cousin Elfroy had been Saint Nicholas's lead helper for a long time."

"Tell them how long," Enya demanded.

"I don't know exactly. Do you?"

"I do," Aeri said.

"Not exactly," Enya replied.

"Aeri said she knew," Ushka interjected.

"Really?" Enya asked.

Aeri nodded. "Yes, Elfroy became the lead helper to St. Nicholas, actually more commonly known as St. Nick or Santa Claus, in the year 1432143. Santa was the Head Honcho Elf, so of course he took other elves as his helpers.

"Oh, yeah! She's right," Enya agreed. "He didn't take pixies, even though elves are our cousins. I don't know why he didn't take pixies."

"Well, I do," Tierri said, "and I'm telling this story! Once they hear it, they'll know why Santa doesn't take pixies as helpers."

I knew Tang always found the pixies' banter "charming," so I leaned over and poked him to stop chuckling. Otherwise it would only encourage them even more.

"You three, sit back down! Tierri, continue from Elfroy . . . Please!" I did my best to command the brood. I could already tell this story was not going to be a short one by any stretch of the imagination.

Enya, Ushka and Aeri took their seats back on the stone hearth, moping just a bit.

Tierri continued. "So Santa and his however many reindeer—it is more than four, I'm pretty sure. Maybe four on each side. Anyway, they landed in *our* glen on the Isle of Gwynf'l right on Christmas Eve. My little sisses had all wandered off to wherever. St. Nicholas—"

"Santa Claus!" Enya jumped up once again and started dancing in circles.

"Papa Noel!" Ushka also jumped up and linked her arm in Enya's to join the dance.

"Cinder Claus!" Aeri did a little jig around the other two.

"Shush, I'm telling this story!" Tierri said again. "St. Nicholas told me that our cousin *Elroy* had taken ill and suggested that he go to the Isle of Gwynf'l and get our assistance."

"That's when we showed up." Ushka had now linked arms with the other two, and the three of them made a ring around Tierri, dancing and shouting every Santa Claus nickname they could come up with. A few were completely obscure or entirely made up.

Once again, I had to interrupt the band of pixies. Otherwise, it would be New Year's Eve before this tale ever got finished. I told the dancing sprites to sit back down and stay seated!

Mat and Nina simply shifted positions to get more comfortable, and pulled the fleece throw closer to them. I wasn't sure if they were just trying to warm themselves, or using the throw cover to dim the "din."

"Tierri, we all now know Santa is also known as St. Nick, etc.," I said. "He told you that Elfroy sent him to get *all* of your help. Tell us what happened next."

"So Santa told me that *Elroy* sent him to find us," Tierri said.

"Yeah, like who the heck was *Elroy?*" Enya asked. I shot her a look, and indeed she remained seated.

"Oh yeah, Elfroy was our cousin," Aeri explained, "but Santa kept saying *Elroy!*"

Ushka jumped in. "Santa told us that there was a gateway that his elves must flow through, and sometimes their names got changed in order to tell them apart."

"Oh yeah, they dropped the 'F' in Elf," Tierri remembered. "Does that make it an F-Bomb?"

That little line started the whole group snickering, including Mat and Nina. Fortunately Tang was not familiar with the innuendo. I gave all of them a piercing look, which temporarily stayed them.

"They changed the names like they did at Rikers Island," Aeri said.

"No," Enya said. "You mean Ellis Island, silly!"

"Shush!" Tierri said for the umpteenth time in the last ten minutes. "Anyway, it doesn't matter, because St. Nick, who by the way is an elf himself, explained to me that all elves who go to the North Pole had to pass through this gateway, and Elfroy or Elroy were one and the same. Santa put his official Elf Seal on it. But Santa seemed a little skeptical about asking for our help."

"He was not!" Enya argued.

Tierri hushed her again. "This is why I'm telling the story, because I'm pretty sure he *was*! So he suggested we try it out by helping him deliver the presents to the fishing village on the Isle."

Aeri squeaked. "This part was cool! Santa and I decided which house we were going to first."

"No, you didn't! Santa had a naughty and nice list for the village." Enya stretched out an imaginary list before her, making little air check marks. "We started with the first one on this list."

"Well, he gave me the doll to place under the tree first. The doll was beautiful, with a light blue satin dress and hair so blond it almost looked white, like mine!" Aeri fluffed at her cloud-like curls.

"He gave me some little ornaments to decorate the tree," Ushka said. "I put a few of my ribbons on the tree too. There was a pretty lake blue one, and a green sea foam colored one."

"He gave me a stocking to hang on the fireplace mantle," Enya said. "There were all kinds of treats in it, even a cinnamon stick! I love cinnamon."

"Well, I hope you didn't take it," Tierri said. Enya kind of turned her head away, maybe feeling a bit guilty. "Anyway, it was a simple job that seemed to go well. So Santa sent us to the next house. This family had a Christmas tree all lit with candles, just like the one we have now.

I was placing the presents under the tree, when we all realized that Aeri wasn't with us."

All of the pixies, except for Aeri, put a hand to their brows and turned their heads to the left then to the right, as if searching for something or someone.

"They sent me back to the first house to go find her," Ushka said. "And I did. There she was still under the tree playing with that little girl's doll."

Aeri stood up and placed her hands on her hips, elbows akimbo. "I wasn't playing with it! I was making sure it wasn't broken."

I motioned for Aeri to sit back down, which she did, still pouting over the accusation.

"Finally, Ushka and Aeri returned to the house with the tree that was lit up with little candles. But then Aeri started to blow out the candles on the tree." Tierri made little puffing sounds to illustrate.

"Yeah, so I had to relight them!" Enya flicked her fingers to demonstrate, which upon the second snap, a tiny flame appeared at her fingertip, and Aeri leapt up to blow it out.

"Ahem!" I loudly cleared my throat, and Aeri sat back down again. That seldom worked, but it did this time.

Tierri continued. "Aeri, as you can tell, gets a little over excited as she did that night and flashed an air blast at the entire tree, and all of the candles went out at once.

"Poof!" Ushka said. "Like magic!"

Tierri nodded. "Then Enya retaliated with a fire blast."

"Boom! The whole tree went up in flames!" Ushka waved her hands wildly above her head, as if flames were shooting from the top of her scalp. "I had to send a water blast at the tree to put the fire out before the whole place burned down. WHOOSH!"

"And now all of the presents under the tree were either scorched or soaking wet or *both*," Tierri went on.

"Or muddy, because you sent a dirt blast on the flames too! Remember?" Ushka pointed out. Now it was Tierri who turned her head away with a bit of a mea culpa look.

"When Santa saw what happened," Aeri said, "he really wasn't too happy. He hustled all of you out but let me stay behind to blow dry the presents and the mud and sweep up the whole mess."

"*I'm* going to tell you about the next house!" Enya stood up, this time ignoring my glare.

"Why?" Tierri demanded. "I'm telling the story!"

"Yeah?" Enya asked. "Well, you were a little pre-occupied, if you remember." Tierri gave a little smirk, but acquiesced and took Enya's seat at the fireplace. "You see, while Santa took off on his sleigh to go to the next rooftop and Aeri stayed behind to do the fire and rescue at the last house, the rest of us ran through the snow to meet up with Santa's next appointed round." Enya did her air check mark again on the mysteriously transparent naughty and nice list.

"This house had a live tree," Tierri said. "It was so elegant. I mean 'live' like not chopped down. In fact, they had already dug a hole in the yard to plant it after Christmas."

"She's right, because I fell in the hole," Ushka remembered, nodding.

"Regardless," Enya continued, "I'm in this house helping St. Nick put all the toys under the tree. This was a big family so there was a lot of work to do. I looked around and noticed I was the only one working here. Tierri was too busy talking to the dang tree!"

Tierri jumped up from her seat to explain. "Well, he was very interesting. I shook hands with him. Well, actually it was just a branch, but he shook it with my hand. He had a lot to tell me. In fact, he used to grow on the edge of our glen, and he said he knew us pixies because he always watched us play there. He said he used to shake his branches to drop pine cones for us, so we could gather the pine nuts. He also told me—"

I had to stop Tierri, as she was getting into her own little world, instead of finishing their Christmas tale. It wasn't unusual for any of the pixies to take off on a tangent, so it was rather remarkable they stayed pretty much on track this evening. "Tierri, sit back down, and let Enya continue. Enya, please tell us about this last house."

"Well, in fact, it *was* the last house. As Ushka mentioned, she fell into the hole that was waiting for the live tree to be planted."

"But don't worry. I didn't get hurt."

"That's because it was filled with snow," Enya explained. "So Ushka did what Ushka does—she played in the snow hole. When Aeri had finished airing things out and sweeping up at the previous stop, she found Ushka in the hole, so she jumped in and started playing with her."

"We made snow angels! They were perfect!" She and Ushka got up from their seats and lay on their backs on the hearth rug, making invisible snow angels.

"Then, holy cow," Tierri said, "the village clock chimed a quarter past midnight!" Aeri and Ushka stopped sweeping their arms along the hearth rug, sat up and started making chiming sounds—*ding, dang, ting, clang*. "Poor Santa still had the rest of the world to deliver presents to before dawn."

"That's when Santa told us that he got a message from Elroy, oops, he meant Elfroy," Enya said. "Elfroy had told him that he was feeling much better and would join him shortly, so Santa could handle things from here."

"He had like a mental telephone thing going on with Elfroy," Aeri said.

Enya laughed. "Mental *telepathy*, ding dong! No wonder you didn't get into the Sun & Moon Academy College of Supernatural Guardians."

Aeri jabbed her finger at her sister. "Neither did you, smarty pants!"

"Hey, none of us did," Ushka said.

"Well, anyway," Enya continued, "Santa and his reindeer took off like a bolt of lightning. Seemed like he was in a real hurry, but he was waving goodbye and wishing us all a good night!"

All four pixies now looked up at an imaginary Santa and waved their hands.

❄

"So that was the night we were Santa's Little Helpers Number 1—" Tierri pointed at herself, then ticked off the other three pixies. "And Number 2, Number 3, and Number 4."

"Just like Thing 1 and Thing 2, but with more Things!" Aeri said, and they all fell into a fit of giggles.

Tang looked at me quizzically, and I briefly explained about Dr. Seuss's *The Cat in the Hat*. I told him I would get him a copy, but actually, since he enjoyed the pixies so much, I had already purchased the book from Sedona at Shelf Indulgence. It was wrapped and waiting for him to open in the morning.

Nina uncurled herself from the fleece and from Mat, stood up, and began applauding, saying "Bravo! Magnifico!"

Mat just burst out laughing, which actually sounded more like hooting, but that was perfectly natural, since he was an owl-shifter. I was glad he held it in this long. Tang Wu stood up, applauded, and bowed to the tiny narrators with his hands together like in prayer, his thanks to the raconteurs.

Cyllene flew off of Tang's shoulder and began circling above the pixie sisters, flapping her luminous wings in applause and buzzing incessantly.

The pixies were so overjoyed with their performance and its reception that they immediately began patting each other on the backs. That, needless to say, turned into rabbit punches, which needless to say again, turned into a wrestling match. I separated the brawling bunch, and introduced our cast to the audience:

"Tierri, Thing One." Tierri took a deep laborious bow. "Enya, Thing Two." Enya jumped up and down, her hands clenched in fists over her head in a champion's stance. "Aeri, Thing Three." Little Aeri curtsied sweetly and did a little twirl. "And of course, Ushka, Thing Four." Ushka bowed quickly several times then began a little victory jig.

I changed my mind about the gift for Tang, and picked it out from underneath the tree and handed it to him right then. The pixies all gathered around him while he delicately unraveled the package to reveal the book.

Enya squealed. "*The Cat in the Hat*! Oh, my favorite!"

"Mine too!" Aeri shrieked.

"Mine three!" Ushka added.

"Mine four!" Tierri finished. "Oh, please, Tang would you read it to us?"

No longer able to suppress it, I yawned loudly. This was far beyond my bedtime already, as Tang knew.

He smiled at the rambunctious imps and said politely, "Well, I think we have had enough story-telling for one night. Perhaps in the morning. Meanwhile, Merry Christmas to all and to all a good night!"

If you haven't already, read about Teeny Weeny and her growing family starting *The Winged & the Wicked* by T.V. Hahn & Kristie Cook

A VERY MERRY MCCABE CHRISTMAS

BY E.J. FECHENDA

A McCabe Family Short Story

*E*verything hurt. Aster rolled over in bed with a groan. Her niece's cries bounced around inside her head like a pinball. She pried an eye open and immediately closed it with a wince as the daylight was way too bright, even with it snowing outside.

"Why do I feel like I went ten rounds in the cage with Ryker last night?" Gage, her mate, asked from where he lay next to her.

"I forgot how potent warded whiskey can be. That was one hell of a wedding last night."

They both sighed in relief when Mina's cries quieted. Aster and Gage along with Aster's sister, Reeve, her mate, and their daughter had come home to Havenwood Falls for the holidays—the first Christmas in two years the McCabe family would celebrate together. The night before they attended Rusty and Sherry's Christmas Eve wedding, and the whiskey flowed a little too freely.

"I want to shut the curtains but I can't move," Aster said, and Gage grunted in agreement. Suddenly, the door to the bedroom burst open, and Aster's nephew came barreling into the room. He flew onto the bed, landing in the middle, where he proceeded to jump up and down. The movement caused Aster's stomach to roll and she gripped the comforter tight, as if she was on a rocking ship and holding on for dear life so she didn't get tossed overboard.

"Auntie Aster, wake up! It's time to open presents!" Jacob squealed.

"Jacob, you leave your aunt alone!" Kaitlyn, Aster's sister-in-law, appeared in the doorway. "Come on, Pop Pop finished making pancakes."

"PANCAKES!" Jacob cheered and leapt off the bed, leaving as quickly as he had entered. Once again, blissful quiet descended upon the room.

"Was that your nephew or a tornado?" Gage asked, making Aster giggle. She turned her head to look at her mate. His blond hair looked like a tornado had gone through it, which meant her red locks were a natural disaster too. He wasn't wearing a shirt, and his muscles were on full display. If she didn't feel like death warmed over, she'd pounce on him for a quickie. Just the thought of moving made her nauseous.

"Oh, shit!" Even though every movement hurt, Aster bolted from bed and ran across the hall to the bathroom, making it to the toilet just in time. The smell of sour whiskey wafted up from the bowl, triggering another round of vomiting. "Ugh," she groaned and rested her forehead on her arm that was draped across the toilet seat. Gage came in behind her and lifted her hair off her back, securing it in a ponytail.

"You okay?" he asked, placing a kiss on top of her head.

"Yeah, feeling better now." She stood up on shaky legs and splashed cool water on her face before brushing her teeth. "No drinking for me for a while."

Gage chuckled. "Even puking your guts out, you're still gorgeous. Shower with me?"

She narrowed her green eyes at him. "I'm not up for shower sex. Rain check, and maybe when my parents aren't in the house?"

"This is just a regular shower. We both smell like a distillery, and we need to hurry before Jacob barges in again. Besides, you have a chunk of something in your hair." Gage scrunched up his face in mock disgust and pointed at the end of her ponytail.

"Oh, gross!" Aster quickly stripped and beat Gage into the shower where he behaved himself...for the most part.

Minutes later, they were downstairs in the kitchen with mugs of piping hot coffee. The sweet scent of maple syrup hung in the air as did the irresistible smell of bacon. Suddenly Aster was ravenous. Bacon grease would cure their hangovers. It was practically medicinal.

With bellies full, Aster and Gage joined her family in the living room where Jacob had finally corralled everyone to open presents, which there were plenty of—it looked like Santa had dropped off his entire sleigh load underneath the Christmas tree. Reeve and Patrick sat on one end of the sectional, their daughter on Reeve's lap. Aster's parents, plus her grandparents, Daniel and Colleen McCabe, sat on the sofa too. Kaitlyn kneeled on the floor next to Jacob. Sitting on the floor near the tree were two newcomers to the McCabe family, who Aster was still getting to know.

Roxy and Remy were two young cougar shifters who had been adopted by Aster's parents while she and Reeve were in Denver. Since Reeve and Aster were banished from town over two years ago, they had missed out on the twins' arrival. The banishment had ended over the summer and the two sisters were adjusting to having their memories back and to the new family dynamic. There was one member who was sorely missed, and each event since their banishment ended marked the first time those events were held without their brother, Braden, and that made his loss all the more painful.

A memory rushed forth of Braden grinning like a fool as Aster struggled with opening a giant present from him. He had taped the entire box, making it impossible to rip the paper off. She had glared at him before shifting slightly, just enough for one hand to transform into a paw, revealing sharp claws, which sliced through the tape with ease. She'd stuck her tongue out at him as his grin faded. This memory caused her to smile even though her throat was tight with emotion. She wasn't going to cry this morning. She would save those tears for later when she was alone to grieve. Her parents already had two years to mourn, and she wanted this holiday to be full of joy for them. They were all together as a family again. Swallowing past the lump, she cleared her throat and went around the room to hug and kiss her family. She eased herself down onto the floor next to Roxy and Remy, who had a plate of sugar cookies on his lap and crumbs clung to the front of his tee shirt.

"Merry Christmas, guys," she said to the twins. Roxy's honey colored eyes met Aster's, and the girl gave her a smile. "Where are Thing 1 and Thing 2?" Aster asked her, referring to Roxy's mates. Yes, mates. Apparently her first semester at the new Sun & Moon Academy Halvard Campus had been life changing and educational on more than an academic level. Aster was twenty-two when she met Gage and felt the mating call. Roxy was only seventeen and felt the call with two men. Usually where Roxy went, so did her mates. Aster was surprised to not see them.

"They're at Whisper Falls Inn, and I'll be meeting up with them later."

Presents were passed around and excited chatter with the background sound of crinkling paper filled the room. Aster's cheeks hurt from laughing, and she got weepy eyed when she opened the present from her parents. It was a collage-style frame full of pictures from her childhood, all from family vacations and many which included Braden.

"It's for your home in Denver," her mom explained. "We had to use pictures not taken here or showing anything identifiable about Havenwood Falls. Otherwise they would fade once you take them past the wards."

"I love it. This is perfect! Thanks, Mom and Dad." Aster stood up and crossed the room to give her parents a hug. The movement triggered another wave of nausea, and she had to rush to the bathroom again. When she opened the door, Gage was waiting for her in the hallway; his blue eyes were focused on her.

"Are you okay?"

"Yeah, this hangover is a bitch. I need some water." He followed her into the kitchen, his gaze still focused on her. "What—do I have puke in my hair again?"

"No. I don't think you're hungover."

"Uh, yeah I am. You and I both."

He shook his head and moved closer, placing his hands on her hips. Leaning down, he nuzzled her neck, and she instantly responded, tilting her head to give him more access. She heard him sniffing her skin before he kissed her right at the juncture where her neck and shoulder met.

"I thought so," he said before tracing kisses along her neck. His hands cupped her ass possessively, and he pulled her against him. She ran her hands up his chest before burying them in his hair. Time ceased to exist as she got lost in the sensations of Gage touching her. She whined slightly when he pulled away, nipping her skin before resting his forehead against hers. "Your scent is different."

"Are you saying I smell? We showered together, remember?" she teased, playing with the back of his neck by running her fingers up and down the closely shorn hairs.

Gage chuckled, and she felt the rumble in his chest; it was similar to his purr, and she pressed herself closer, absorbing the vibration.

"I think you're pregnant, my mate, my love," he said softly before kissing her forehead.

"What?" Aster stepped out of his embrace and came to an abrupt stop when her back hit the counter. She placed a hand on her stomach. "What makes you think that?"

"Babe," Gage said, moving forward to close the distance between them. "Your scent is different. I noticed it last week but didn't think anything of it because we were busy and you were stressed out buying presents for your family. The change is more noticeable now—stronger, sweeter." He bent his head, dragging his lips along her neck as he inhaled deeply.

Aster clutched at her flat stomach. She didn't feel different. Her breasts had been tender but that was normal during PMS, which...she counted backwards in her head to the last time she had her period. Oh, crap. She was well over three weeks late. Gage was right that she had been busy and not really paying attention. They hadn't been trying to get pregnant, but they hadn't been trying to prevent it either. They were mated and knew they'd have children or cubs eventually.

"Shit." She dropped her head against Gage's shoulder. "If I am, I've been drinking." Another wave of nausea loomed at this thought, but she choked it down, and the wave receded.

"Relax, baby, I'm sure you're fine."

"But I need to know for sure." Aster gnawed on her bottom lip as guilt consumed her. If she was pregnant, she was already failing as a mother. Unlike Reeve, who was the picture of wholesomeness the entire time she was carrying Mina. She made organic protein shakes practically every morning, consuming more nuts and berries than was natural for a mountain lion shifter. Aster winced at the negative direction of her thoughts. The days of comparing herself to her sister and thinking she wasn't as perfect and good were over, but it was like a default mode that kicked in occasionally. She loved Reeve. Any animosity or jealousy she felt toward her sister when they were younger didn't exist anymore.

"When we get back to Denver, we'll go see the den doctor, okay?" Gage moved so Aster had to lift her head, and she met his steady gaze.

"No, I need to know now."

"Today?" Gage laughed. "It's Christmas."

"Oh, right," Aster huffed, blowing a strand of hair that had drifted free of her ponytail. "Tomorrow, then, but I don't want to go to the medical center. Word will spread through town faster than wildfire. I want to keep this quiet until we know for sure." She lowered her voice, knowing how sensitive her family's hearing was. Although the noise coming from the living room provided enough cover, it only took one curious cat to listen in.

"Where will we go?" Gage asked. A line formed between his eyebrows as his face scrunched up in confusion.

"Paisley will be able to tell. She's home from school for winter break. I'll reach out to her." Paisley Underwood's dad was one of the doctors at the medical center, and she was following in his footsteps. She was fae and had inherited his healing abilities. Aster had witnessed

Paisley's skills in action over the summer when Paisley had healed a severe burn on Aster's hand—had healed it within seconds.

"Sounds like a plan, and even though I want to shout it to the world, I'll be quiet." He winked and lowered his mouth to hers, but she jerked away at the last minute.

"Gross! I just puked!"

Gage laughed at her horrified expression, and that's when Aster's mom, Anne, walked in, holding a dirty coffee mug in each hand.

"What are you two doing hiding out in the kitchen? There are presents to be unwrapped," she said, setting the mugs on the granite countertop. Aster just smiled at her mom and grabbed Gage's hand, pulling him out of the room before either of them broke and shared their suspicions about Aster's condition.

After opening presents, the family sat around the roaring fireplace. Snow had been steadily falling all morning, and everyone seemed content to stay inside. Coffee was replaced with cocktails, which Aster passed on, using her "hangover" as an excuse. Afternoon cocktails rolled into a prime rib dinner with enough sides to feed a football team. Aster practically drooled on herself as her dad carved slices of prime rib; she watched the tantalizing slow drip of blood as the juices collected on the platter underneath the roast. Her stomach growled so loud, her grandfather heard it at the other end of the table. Any nausea from earlier was gone, and all Aster wanted was the rarest slices of meat. She whined when her dad sopped up the juices with a roll.

"What's gotten into you, kiddo?" he asked her. "This always grossed you out." Her eyes tracked the movement like it was prey when he popped the dripping roll into his mouth.

"Nothing. That just looked really tasty."

Her dad laughed and shook his head, laugh lines fanned out around his blue eyes. "You and your sister are always keeping me guessing."

He winked and turned his attention to Jacob, who had appeared at his side with an empty plate in hand, looking for more food.

Dessert followed dinner, and by the time dishes were loaded in the dishwasher, Aster thought she was going to get a cramp, she was so full. Darkness had descended upon the box valley. She stood at the sliding glass doors that led to the back deck and stared up at the stars peeking through a light cloud cover. The snow had tapered off into a cold night.

"It's gorgeous out," her sister said, coming to stand beside her. "We're going to shift and go for a run in the fresh powder. Coming?"

Aster looked over her shoulder and saw her family getting ready to leave—everyone except her sister-in-law who held a forlorn looking Jacob by his hand. She was quietly explaining to him that he wasn't old enough to shift yet and it was almost his bedtime.

Realizing she couldn't shift either, if she was indeed pregnant, she approached her sister-in-law. "I'll stay and get Jacob ready for bed. I'll watch Mina, too," she said to Reeve. "I'm still out of sorts from the wedding and don't feel up for a shift."

Reeve's eyebrow rose in a sharp arch. "Are you sure?"

"Yeah, positive. You all go and have fun. I got this." She grabbed Jacob's other hand, and he smiled up at her.

Everyone started to file out of the kitchen through the garage. It was a ten-minute drive to the nearest thatch of woods where they could shift in private. Gage hung back and kissed Aster goodbye.

"See, you're already thinking like a mom," he whispered in her ear, gently spanning his palm across her stomach. "See you soon."

About an hour later, Aster was stretched out alongside her nephew on the sofa, reading him a Dr. Seuss book. He yawned and cuddled in closer against her. Then she yawned, and within moments, both were fast asleep. She woke at one point when Gage came in and scooped her up to carry her into their room.

When she woke the next morning, sunlight streamed in, and she didn't have the same aversion to daylight as the day before. Icicles hanging off the eaves sparkled outside the window. She looked over at her mate. Gage was sprawled out on his side of the bed. He had kicked his blanket off at some point and lay on his back snoring slightly. She hated to wake him up, especially since he had probably been out late, but he wanted to go with her to see Paisley. A nervous flutter erupted inside her belly, and she placed her palm against her stomach to settle it. Soon she would know for sure if she was pregnant. She rolled onto her side, so she was facing Gage and rose up on her elbow. Nudging him awake, she watched as he peered up at her, his blue eyes slightly bloodshot.

"Morning, sleepyhead," she said and smiled before leaning down to kiss him. "Paisley said to come by around ten. That gives us an hour to get ready."

It was like she zapped him with a cattle prod; he was up and out of bed, pulling on jeans before she blinked. After buttoning his jeans, he looked over at her with his eyebrows raised. "What are you still doing in bed? Let's go!"

Aster snorted and shook her head, then swung her legs over the side of the bed. Gage's enthusiasm was contagious, but she was hesitant to get wrapped up in it. What if he was wrong and she wasn't pregnant? The disappointment would be crushing. She didn't realize how much she wanted a baby, and apparently Gage did too.

They went downstairs to a quiet house. The coffee pot was still on, but Aster opted for a glass of apple cider.

"Just in case, right?" she said when Gage gave her a surprised look. For her, coffee was life and a necessity every morning. "Remember Reeve had to watch the caffeine."

"Oh, right." He poured a mug for himself and set the pot back on the maker.

"Did I hear my name?" Reeve asked, wandering into the kitchen. She was still in her pajamas, her red hair pulled back in a messy ponytail. She held Mina in her arms. Motherhood had changed Reeve. She used to shower and get dressed first thing in the morning.

Nowadays she was happy to find a clean shirt, let alone one that was ironed to a crisp.

"I was just making sure Gage left you some coffee. I figured you'd need the caffeine."

"You're a goddess. Little miss was raring to go early this morning and after last night's run, I didn't get much sleep."

"Where is everyone?" Aster asked.

"Patrick didn't hear Mina fussing, so I took one for the team and let him sleep in. Mom and Dad had some business to deal with, and Kaitlyn took Jacob home. Roxy spent the night at the inn, and Remy is still sleeping. Where are you guys off to?" Reeve's eyes scanned them, realizing they were dressed to go out.

"Oh, um," Aster stammered, hating having to lie to her sister. "We're going to stop by Paisley's and deliver her Christmas present."

Reeve narrowed her green eyes at Aster and tilted her head to the side. "You're being weird."

"No, I'm not." Aster broke eye contact and hurried across the room to the kitchen sink where she rinsed her glass out before setting it in the dishwasher.

"Yeah you are. You didn't want to go for a run last night, and you were acting weird yesterday, too." Aster didn't say anything but felt her sister staring at her back. She cleared her throat and turned to leave. "Wait. When are you coming back? We're supposed to go to the cemetery today, remember?" Reeve asked.

Aster stopped and looked over at her sister. She had forgotten and guilt took the form of tears that threatened to spill. They had made plans to visit their brother's grave. How could she have forgotten? "I'll meet you there at noon, and then we'll grab lunch together. Okay?"

"Fine. I'll meet you at the gate. Don't be late."

Sand crunched underfoot as Aster and Gage walked hand in hand along the winding sidewalks of Creekwood, which had iced over the night before. Snow covered everything, and the neighborhoods had been transformed into a winter wonderland that would last until March or April. Fresh, cold air numbed her nose and made her face feel tight. Aster breathed it in, enjoying the cooling sensation on her lungs and all of the scents that surrounded her. While her sense of smell was at its best when she was in her mountain lion form, she still had enhanced senses in her human form and could smell the decay of leaves buried beneath the blanket of snow.

Paisley lived a couple streets over from Aster's childhood home, and they opted to walk over. The Underwoods' house stood out on the street because it was the only one that had flowers still blooming. Red roses peeked out from underneath snow, looking like splashes of blood. Paisley's mom owned Fairy Tale Florists and had the ability to make flora and fauna thrive in extreme conditions.

"That's really cool," Gage commented as they walked up the driveway. He stopped to smell the roses. "I'm surprised the Court lets her get away with it," he added, referring to the government that enforced strict policy and rules to keep the supernatural residents a secret from the human residents.

"It's glamoured so only supes can see them," Aster explained.

Before Aster could ring the doorbell, Paisley swung the door wide open. "Come in! I can't wait to get started. We need to find out if you're prego!"

Paisley ushered them inside where they peeled off their winter coats and took off their boots. The scent of balsam was overwhelming, and Aster followed her nose to the source. The Underwood's Christmas tree in the living room was an actual live tree. It had literally sprouted up through the floor and was decorated with all silver and white ornaments. Red poinsettias filled every corner of the room.

"Wow!" Gage said, staring in amazement.

"Yeah, my mom goes a little overboard every year. Come on." She tugged on Aster's sleeve, pulling her toward the stairs that led to the second floor. "I figured my bedroom is the best place to do this."

"Are you the only one here?" Aster asked.

"Yup. Dalton is snowboarding, and my dad is at the medical

center. Mom had to go in the shop to fill some orders. You have the privacy you requested."

"Perfect." Aster and Gage followed Paisley up the stairs and down the carpeted hallway to her bedroom. That's when Aster noticed her friend's hair color was different in the back than the white blond in the front. Paisley was always experimenting with her glamour and changing her highlights in her pixie cut. This time around, Paisley had gone festive. The hair on the back of her head was a swirl of red and green.

"Okay, lay down on your back with your head at the foot of my bed," Paisley instructed, taking charge and assuming a more professional tone. Aster complied and looked up at the strands of tiny white lights that hung from the ceiling.

"I've learned to diagnose a lot faster this past semester," Paisley said, placing her hands on Aster's temples.

"The Academy sounds really cool. I wish it was around when I was in college." Aster had earned her business degree through an online program. The Sun & Moon Academy's Halvard Campus, a college of supernatural guardians, didn't exist until this past summer. Paisley was a member of the inaugural class.

As warmth began to radiate from Paisley's fingertips and into Aster's temples, she closed her eyes. Paisley had explained her process to her before and said it was similar to reiki. She scanned the body from head to toe, and it was almost like she could see inside.

Paisley gasped, and that caused Aster's eyes to pop open.

"What is it?" she asked peering up at her friend, meeting her violet eyes.

"You, my cat friend, are definitely pregnant, and the fetus is healthy. Just lay off the warded whiskey from this point on," Paisley said with a giggle.

Aster breathed out a sigh of relief and turned her head to find Gage beaming down at her. She sat up slowly, the shock and disbelief making her movements slow, like she wasn't connected with her body. As soon as she stood, Gage pulled her into his arms.

"We're having a baby," she whispered against his chest, getting used to the words.

"We're having a baby," Gage echoed, sounding more confident.

They were almost at her parents' house before the shock wore off. Aster barely remembered saying goodbye to Paisley, who had the sense to give Gage a list of prenatal instructions and supplements to pick up at Howe's Herbal Shoppe.

"We're having a baby," she said again, and Gage laughed, a pleased chuckle, and she noticed he was walking with his chest puffed out.

"Yes, we are, my love. My mate," he said with a slight growl and lifted her gloved hand to his lips. That's when she noticed the time.

"Shit! I'm late meeting Reeve."

Gage pulled his keys out of his pocket. "Get in, I'll drop you off."

He opened the passenger door to his truck, and Aster climbed in. She tried texting Reeve that she was on her way, but the texts weren't going through. Havenwood Falls had the most unreliable cell service.

It took less than ten minutes to reach the cemetery, which was located off of Blackstone Road and connected to Cook's Corner Park. Reeve stood by the arched wrought-iron sign that marked the entrance to the cemetery, which was one-part English garden and one-part labyrinth in the summer, where columns of wisteria and rows of bushes took over. Now everything beyond the gate had been tamed by winter.

Gage pulled up to the curb, and Reeve stopped her pacing when she saw them.

"I'll see you later," Aster said to Gage. "I'm going to tell Reeve the news. Patrick is your beta, so you should tell him, and we'll tell my parents together—tonight."

"Sounds good." Gage leaned over the console, and they kissed, slow and sweet, without the usual spark of animalistic lust. This was a kiss to treasure, one that spoke of love and devotion. He cupped her cheek, and she melted into his touch. When they broke apart, they didn't move away. "You be careful and call me if you need anything," he whispered.

"I will, babe. I love you."

"Love you more," he said and kissed her forehead before releasing her cheek.

Aster got out of the truck and made her way to Reeve, leaving a path of fresh footprints in the snow.

"I almost left," her sister snapped at her, but Aster didn't take it personally. Reeve always acted angry and out of sorts before visiting Braden's grave. Where their parents had two years to grieve and cope with his death, the banishment had wiped those memories away, so Aster and Reeve were still dealing with raw grief, and they both shared guilt in how he died—defending and protecting them. Aster reached for her sister's hand and gave it a reassuring squeeze. Together they passed through the gate and entered the cemetery. They had to go through the human section first. This was the public section, and the paths were well maintained, shoveled, and salted—even the stone benches were cleared of snow. They were silent as they walked past neat rows of evenly spaced headstones, some of which were aged by the elements, the stone weathered to a dark gray and stained with streaks of black from decades of moisture.

At the back of the public part of the cemetery, there was a separate trail that led to a stone arch, an entrance to a tunnel that went underneath Blackstone Road. They continued through the narrow passage that opened up to the supernatural part of the cemetery. It was almost like stepping through time. Hulking mausoleums for the founding families took up one side of the cemetery, and the landscape wasn't as well maintained as the human section. It was easy to tell which graves dated back to before the twentieth century as they had gothic metal cages over them—cages intended to contain the dead who might happen to rise again. It was easy to spot Braden's grave as it was one of the newer ones. Many of the gravestones had runes or magical symbols etched in them. Braden's had an impression of a large paw print pressed into the gravestone below his name. The inscription was simple:

Braden Michael McCabe
March 30, 1987 – June 12, 2017
Son – Brother – Father
Forever Loyal

"Christmas was yesterday." Reeve broke the silence, her voice sounding thick, and Aster glanced over to see tears were already running down her sister's face. "It was so weird not having you there. You should have seen Jacob." Reeve sniffed and stopped talking.

"He couldn't wait to open presents." Aster picked up the conversation. "He looks so much like you, Braden, more so every day. He even has your laugh."

"I wish you were here. I wish you could see your niece, Mina. She has red hair too." Reeve had recovered enough to speak again. "I'm so sorry you're not here."

Aster put her arm around Reeve's back, and the two sisters leaned into each other, supporting each other's weight, sharing the burden of grief. They stayed like that for a few moments of solemn reflection until a sharp cry from a hawk flying above pierced the silence.

"I have something to share, and I wanted you to hear it first," Aster said to Reeve, but she was also talking to Braden. Perhaps he was out there somewhere listening.

"What?"

"I'm pregnant."

"What!" Reeve stepped away from Aster and turned to look at her. "Are you serious?"

Aster nodded, and Reeve's face transformed. A giant smile erased any traces of sadness. "My baby sister is having a baby. Oh my god, how long have you known? How far along are you? Why didn't you say anything?"

"I'm saying something now, and I only just found out. That's why we went to see Paisley. You're the first to know. Well, besides Gage and Paisley."

"This is incredible news!" Aster was pulled into another hug, and she laughed at her sister's enthusiasm.

"If the baby's a boy, I want to name him Braden," Aster blurted out. She was still adjusting to the concept of being pregnant and wasn't anywhere close to picking out names, but the idea appeared out of the blue and it felt right.

"Oh, sis, that's perfect!" Reeve hugged Aster more fiercely. By the time they separated, both of them had tears running down their cheeks.

"Braden, if you're listening, you will live on in us. You will never be forgotten," Aster declared. She kissed her fingertips before placing them on top of his gravestone.

"We'll be back to check in," Reeve promised. "Now Aster and I are going to Coffee Haven. We'll have a blueberry scone in your memory since those were your favorite."

The two sisters left, and as they were getting ready to go through the tunnel, Aster saw something out of the corner of her eye that caught her attention, something she hadn't noticed when they arrived. Next to a stone bench located just steps from the path they were on, a statue of an angel had fallen on its side. Aster bent down, and when she set the angel upright, noticed something else. In the untouched snow in front of the bench, there was a single paw print. There weren't any other prints around, which was strange. And it wasn't just any paw print, but one from a mountain lion. Chills ran up Aster's spine, and she looked up at Reeve to see if she had noticed. Reeve's eyes glittered with tears.

"Do you think?" Aster asked, and she didn't have to say anything more as her sister apparently had the same thought.

"That has to be a sign from Braden."

Aster stood with a hand pressed against her belly. "You know what? Let's skip Coffee Haven. Mom and Dad should be home by now."

The urge to be with her family came on sudden and strong. She didn't want to wait until that night to tell her parents the happy news. It was time to spread some joy.

Read about the McCabe Family in *Fate, Love & Loyalty* and *Forever Loyal.*

NEW YEAR, NEW LIFE

BY NADIRAH FOXX

An Oscar & Gloriana Short Story

GLORIANA

*I*t took two years to get to this point, my wedding day. Christmas came and went before Oscar Vega popped the question. I'd been hinting at it with no success. I thought attending Izzie and Hunter's wedding would have sparked the idea with the hellhound, but it didn't. Then, when Pandora—a Shinigami death spirit—came to town and moved in with Montezuma Tayute, I thought that would be the impetus. Still nothing.

Then, I told the big lug that he would be a father.

Oscar's whole demeanor changed. Suddenly, he wanted the picket fence, the kid, the dog. He finally wanted to slip that ring on my finger. I didn't complain. Just wondered what took so long.

I would have been content with a simple ceremony at the Court of the Sun and the Moon—or at the Swords of the Infernal Night clubhouse. My fiancé wouldn't hear of it. He said he wasn't doing the deed twice. It was why I was nervous as hell waiting in an upstairs room of Whisper Falls Inn.

Actually, it was a perfect time for a wedding. Although I wasn't a fan of all the snow and ice, it was beautiful in Havenwood Falls. There was always something going on in town. Another wedding seemed like the right way to end the year.

Our friends gathered in the library, which Michaela had turned into the perfect wedding site with calla lilies and purple irises. The same cream and purple combination made up the bouquet in my hands. I didn't care about the décor. I was only happy that Callie's Consignments had a dress big enough to go over my baby bump.

Someone knocked at the door.

"Come in."

It opened, and a girl with midnight-brown hair appeared. "How's it going? Ready?"

Smiling, I said, "I think so. Do I look okay?"

Izzie James, formerly Izzie Itzae, came over to the full-length mirror and stared at my reflection. She pushed an errant black curl off my bare shoulder. "You look beautiful. Oscar will love it."

There was another knock, and we turned to the sound.

My smile immediately turned upside down. The one face I wasn't happy to see stood in the doorway. He should not have been there. He was the reason I left Spain—left my family. The flowers I held shook.

"Gloriana?" asked Izzie.

I had to admit he was handsome even for a Cuélebra, but then again, he was part snake and part dragon. It was their appearance that snared their prey. I, however, wasn't Alejandro Veleta's quarry. The male was my ex. Well, he would have been my ex had I returned the ring.

Clearing my throat, I said, "Izzie meet Alejandro Veleta. He came all the way from northern Spain."

"Oh? Is he family?"

"No. He was my fiancé."

Good thing Izzie wasn't eating or drinking. Instead, she choked on her words.

"I beg to differ," Alejandro said as he came farther into the room. "What you imply is only true if we broke the engagement. Last time I checked, you still had my ring."

Izzie blurted, "Maybe I should give you a minute?"

"Yeah. Thanks." I gripped the chair beside me and took a deep breath.

Mama must have told him I was getting married. Alejandro wore a tailored black suit with a matching shirt and tie. Nobody looked as good in black as that male—except for Oscar.

"If you're here to collect, I don't have the ring. I pawned it a couple of years ago."

He ignored my comment, and his gaze went to my stomach. "It seems you've been occupied."

"I was living my life."

"It wasn't yours to live," he stated flatly. "Have you forgotten the agreement?"

Actually, I had. I came from a small village in Spain. Centuries ago, a breed of creature known as Cuélebras descended upon the villagers. The snake-like dragons promised not to devour anyone if a pact could be reached. The elders sat down with one of the beasts by the last name Veleta. A promise was made that as each of the Veleta sons matured, they would take a wife chosen from the villagers. A lottery was held to determine which families would participate. My family's name was chosen, and I was promised to Alejandro—a fourth-born daughter for a fourth-born son.

Instead of fulfilling my destiny, I ran, and I didn't stop until I had reached America. Eventually, I made my way to Colorado and bumped into Oscar. When he brought me to Havenwood Falls, I forgot all about the promise made to the Veleta family.

"Alejandro, if you haven't noticed, I'm pregnant. I'm marrying the father today."

"This saddens me, Gloriana. You so easily broke your vow to me. Perhaps my family should break its vow to the villagers? When the survivors—if there are any—ask the details, I can tell them that they have you to thank."

I swallowed hard. Dread turned to panic as I heard Oscar's voice outside the door.

❄

OSCAR

Seeing your bride before saying your vows was supposedly bad luck. Maybe there was something to that old superstition because seeing another man, a stranger, in the room with Gloriana spelled all sorts of trouble. She was fucking beautiful, but my eyes couldn't leave the fool in the suit.

"Gloriana, you okay?" I asked, shutting the door behind me.

I expected her to rush over. Put her arms around me. Assure me that I had nothing to worry about. She did none of that. Instead, tears shone in her eyes. Slowly, Gloriana lowered herself to the chair she stood beside. No words. Not one damn word from her.

"Excuse me, partner. Who the hell are you?"

The Antonio Banderas look-alike had the nerve to grin. "My name is Alejandro Veleta. I'm an old *friend* of Gloriana's."

"Really? So, you're from Denver?"

The asshole laughed. "I'm not sure what your bride has told you, but we're both from northern Spain. Her family works for mine."

I glanced at my bride-to-be, looking for clarity.

She muttered, "It's true."

Lie number one.

Jerking my thumb toward Veleta, I asked, "Is he really a friend?"

Gloriana shook her head. "More like my ex. We were to marry."

Lie number two.

"It seems that my fiancée needed some time to think over our engagement. I allowed her to come to America. We waited for her to return home, but she never did. I've been searching for her for two long years."

Lie number three.

What else had she lied about?

My gaze bounced from the mother of my unborn child to the bastard disrupting our wedding day. The tuxedo Izzie talked me into was suddenly too tight. The collar cut off my breathing while my vision turned red. I needed air. Lots of it.

In the distance, I heard Gloriana calling my name as I rushed out the front door of the inn.

"Gunner!" It was Axel.

When I looked up, the nagual shifter was standing beside me on the curb.

"What's going on?"

I pursed my lips, wanting a cigarette, but I quit because it wasn't good for the baby. I'd changed my whole life around for someone who was less than honest with me. "I've been living a fucking lie, Axel. If you ever think about marrying Pandora, make sure you know what you're getting into."

"Fellas, I'm all for fresh air, but it's too damned cold for this," said Hunter James, stopping on the other side of me.

Making sure my shades were in place, I faced him. "Then take yo' ass back inside. I didn't ask for either of you to come out here."

Axel spoke right over me as if I wasn't there. "Something's happened. Can you check on Gloriana?"

"Yeah. Somebody should," I said and then stepped off the curb. Honestly, I didn't know where I was going. The snow crunched beneath the shiny shoes I wore. Maybe I'd go home and change my clothes. Then drink myself into oblivion.

GLORIANA

I couldn't believe what had just happened. "That wasn't your truth to tell!"

Alejandro took a seat on the sofa. "Apparently, it wasn't yours either. If it had been, you would have told him long before he knocked you up."

The door swung open. Hunter and Izzie along with Monte and

Pandora rushed in. Four pairs of eyes landed on me and then noticed the stranger in the room.

Monte, matching Alejandro's height, said, "Who the hell are you?"

My ex lifted an eyebrow as if he was asking permission to speak. Not again.

"Alejandro Veleta meet Monte, Hunter, Izzie, and Pandora. Guys this is my ex," I said wearily.

"Ex?" Izzie said. "How much of an ex are we talking?"

"Gloriana is my fiancée." Alejandro folded his arms over his broad chest.

"Where's Oscar?" I asked.

Rather than answer my question, Monte pointed to the door. "I think it's time for you to leave."

My ex shook his head. "I'm not leaving without what is due me."

Izzie shouted, "Can you not see that Gloriana is pregnant? It's not your baby!"

Stretching out on the sofa, Alejandro said, "She is free to marry whoever she pleases as long as she returns my engagement ring."

Everyone looked at me.

I felt like such a fool. "When I came to this country, I didn't have much. I left nearly everything I had behind just to get away from him. Before I met Oscar, I was flat broke. The ring was all I had left, so I pawned it. I used the funds to get a new identity. I bought a bike too."

Hunter ran a hand through his perfectly coiffed hair. "How much was the ring worth?"

"I got about five grand for it."

Alejandro scoffed. "It was worth more than that. The ring had been in my family for generations."

"Dollar amount, Veleta?" said Hunter.

"At least a million."

Somehow, I doubted if that was the actual number.

The shifter didn't even flinch, but then again, Hunter was an accountant. He was accustomed to dealing with huge sums. "Let me get it straight. If Gloriana returned your property, she can marry Oscar."

"Yes."

"Would you settle for the money?" he asked.

Alejandro cocked his head to one side. "If that is the best that can be done, I'll take it."

Hunter clasped his hands behind his back and began pacing. "Here's what will happen. Monte, can you find Addie? We need to register this fool."

"On it." Monte dashed out of the room.

"Second, Izzie will take Gloriana back to our house. Pandora, let the wedding party know that there's been a change in venue."

I pushed to my feet. "I need to find Oscar."

"As soon as I'm done with this intruder, I'll look for him." He glanced at my ex before reaching into his suit coat jacket. Hunter removed a pen and his checkbook.

"No! You can't pay for my mistake," I shouted.

"Think of it as a wedding present." He scribbled across the page. "Besides, I'll get it back. Veleta, this is temporary. I will check the pawn shops in Denver. If your ring is still there, I will get it to you. If not, keep the check." Hunter handed it to Alejandro.

"Are you good for it?"

"Probably more so than you are."

Someone cleared their throat. We all looked up and saw Addie Beaumont with her trusty messenger bag. "I understand that someone needs to be registered."

Hunter pointed to Alejandro. "When you're done with him, make sure he checks into the inn. He needs to stay close until I can finish some research."

Addie nodded and sat beside Alejandro. As she began unpacking her tools of the trade, Izzie ushered me out of the room.

OSCAR

I practically ripped the damn tie from around my neck. I was a fool to believe that Gloriana was the real deal. Wrongfully, I trusted her. Thought she cared about me. But she couldn't even be honest.

Opening the fridge, I pulled out a brew. Suddenly, I remembered the last time the two of us had a beer together. Gloriana didn't even finish hers. She said it tasted off. Then, she seemed to be tired all the time. Gloriana cancelled her classes at the gym and had Pandora fill in for her. When her *illness* seemed to get worse, I suggested she get off her feet.

"How you feeling?" I tossed my gym bag in the closet and then sat on the side of the bed.

"About the same."

Lowering my glasses, I asked, "Then, why the smile?"

"I know we said that we'd wait a bit before getting married. Maybe we should reconsider moving up that timetable."

Raking a hand over my face, I groaned. "Ah, Glori, I thought we said no rushing down the aisle."

It was something my parents had done, and their marriage didn't last. I didn't want to follow in my father's footsteps.

The smile on her face grew. "But we should probably do it within the next seven months or so."

"What are you talking about?"

"You're going to be a father."

"Say what?" My jaw dropped.

"We're really having a baby." She reached over and placed my hand on her stomach.

"We're... Seriously? There's a little one in there?"

"Yes!"

I forgot all about my parents' shoddy history. I wanted my child to have my last name and wasted no time proposing.

And I told everyone I knew about the pregnancy even though Gloriana said it was too soon.

Did she think it was too soon because of her commitment to Veleta?

I tossed back the beer. Then I heard the front door close.

GLORIANA

Izzie was a good person. She ignored Hunter's demand and brought me home. I had a feeling that I'd find the broody hellhound there. The tie on the floor was proof. Hearing the bottle crash to the floor was confirmation.

"Gloriana, do you want me—"

"I'm good. Go back and make our apologies. This might take a while."

She gave me a hug and then left.

I had made the mess, and only I could clean it up.

Oscar met me halfway. "I'll sleep at the club. You can—"

"No." I grasped his beefy arm with both hands. "I'm going to talk. You're going to listen."

He barreled past me. For a split second, I thought Oscar was leaving. Instead, he parked his butt on his favorite recliner in the living room.

"I have questions."

"Ask away." I sat down on the coffee table and faced him.

"What's the agreement with Veleta?"

Exhaling loudly, I summoned strength I didn't feel. "I come from a small town in northern Spain. We're a family of witches sworn to look after another family. One made up of hideous creatures."

"Like?"

"Cuélebras. They're nasty serpent-like dragons who live high in the mountains. For each son born to the family, they choose a female to be his bride."

"An arranged marriage?"

"Sort of. Females are conceived with that purpose in mind.

Cuélebras are fruitful beasts having many offspring at once. I am the fourth daughter born to Emilio Rodriguez. My destiny was to become Alejandro Veleta's bride."

"So, you ran," Oscar added. "Then you met me and found an easy target."

"No." I reached for his hand, but he pulled away. "You have never been easy."

"Why me? Why string me along?"

My gaze flickered to the ceiling. *"¡Dios mío!* Do you hear yourself? I have been with you for two years. Two long years. We've had our ups and downs. I've been your old lady. I've been your right hand."

"My better half," he muttered.

"Yes! You've been my rock."

"Then why didn't you tell me about all of this?"

"Honestly? I forgot! My love for you is so intense that I easily blot out the world around me." I stood in front of him, waiting for his response.

Finally, Oscar's huge hands wrapped around my ever-expanding waist. Settling onto his lap, I rested my head against his shoulder.

He rubbed my arm. "So where do we go from here?"

"Well, Hunter paid off Alejandro."

"What the fuck!" Oscar moved so fast, I practically toppled onto the floor. He quickly steadied me. "Sorry, Glori. How much do I owe him?"

"A cool mill."

Oscar growled.

"Actually, I think that Alejandro lied. I got about five grand for the ring when I pawned it. He claimed it was worth more."

"Any way to prove it?"

"Hunter will check the pawn stores around Denver to see if it's still there." Sitting up, I said, "But I have a better idea."

"What?"

"I remember the ring. I could create a replica. One that would be hard for Alejandro to detect right away. Hunter would keep his money, and Alejandro would be history."

"Until he discovered the truth, Glori. Then we're right back in the same shit."

"Maybe not."

Oscar tilted his head. "What are you thinking?"

"After we get married, I'm due a honeymoon."

His cheeks reddened. "I knew I was forgetting something."

Ordinarily, I'd be upset, but his forgetfulness might be helpful. "Let's take the opportunity and leave Havenwood Falls."

"Why? This is my home."

"Do you really want to be here when Alejandro comes back? He's part snake, part dragon, part *brujo*, and all mean when crossed."

"Where would we go?"

"Leave that to me." I leaned in and kissed Oscar's full lips. "Baby, I love you, and I can't wait to marry you. Right now, there's a group of our friends waiting at Hunter's house."

Oscar grinned. "You're kidding. What happened to the inn?"

"Nothing. I think Hunter wanted us to put some distance between us and the drama of today."

Suddenly, my husband-to-be stood. "Let's get you married then."

Even without all the decorations, the ceremony was everything I'd hoped for. Izzie and Hunter provided heat lamps on their back deck so that Baba could perform the ceremony outside. Someone had brought all the flowers from the original venue. Izzie was my matron of honor while Hunter was Oscar's best man.

Baba had us stand in a circle. In the center he placed a red candle. "This represents the fire of love that burns brightly in your hearts. This love sustains you and will be a constant inspiration to you and all who know and love you. Please join hands."

When we asked Baba to marry us, it was with the understanding that it would include some Maya traditions. Not a problem. As I told Oscar, it was good to have some traditions even if we borrowed them from others.

Hunter's grandfather began chanting in his native language. Then he said, "Oscar Vega and Gloriana Rodriguez, shelter each other. Warm each other. Be each other's companions. You are two persons, but there is only one life before you. As you journey through life, may beauty surround you. Be happy. Be good together as long as you walk the earth. Respect each other with tenderness, gentleness, and kindness." Baba almost finished without our exchange. "I believe the couple have vows to say."

Oscar pulled out a sheet of paper from his tuxedo pocket. He gave me a smile before reading, "Glori, you know I'm a man of few words. Frankly, there are none that come close to telling you how much I love you. Bruja, you're everything to me. Earlier, my stupidity got in the way, but I promise you that I'm not walking away. Ever. You're mine, baby. I challenge anyone to doubt it."

I wiped the tears streaming down my face. What I had to say couldn't be contained to a sheet of paper. "Oh, Oscar, I love you so much. You understand me better than I know myself. You love me unconditionally. You even tolerate my messiness and nearly burning down the house. Oscar, you are the air that I breathe. You bring me joy every day that I'm with you. And when something separates us, I can't wait to be with you again. I love you and look forward to spending the rest of my days with you."

Baba smiled and watched as Hunter produced a ring. He handed it to Oscar. "Repeat after me, Oscar. With this ring, I thee wed."

It was a beautiful piece of jewelry. A silver band with diamonds, sapphires, and rubies. "With this ring, I thee wed."

Izzie passed me Oscar's ring—an obsidian band embedded with tiny diamonds.

"Gloriana, repeat after me. With this ring, I thee wed."

It took a little push to get the jewelry over his thick finger. "With this ring, I thee wed."

Baba closed his book and said, "As the Great Father commands, you are now man and wife."

Oscar's arms wrapped around me, and he claimed my lips. Slanting his mouth, he deepened the kiss.

Someone called out, "All right, you two. Let the first kid be born before working on number two!"

I broke off the kiss and glanced around the room. Savage was in the back of the room with a wide grin on his face.

The next few minutes blurred by. There were tons of congratulations, and plenty of females wanting to touch my baby bump. When I saw Izzie duck outside, I seized the opportunity.

Closing the sliding door behind me, I said, "Hey, got a minute?"

"Of course. What's up?"

"You're from back east, right?"

"Yup. New York City." Izzie pulled her coat closed. "You know I hated the snow growing up there. I swore I'd find a warm clime when I grew up. Then I ended up here."

"Sometimes fate intervenes despite our best plans."

Izzie's eyebrows knitted together. "What's going on, Gloriana?"

"I have an idea to get rid of Alejandro and keep Hunter from paying him."

"What is it?"

"I can recreate the engagement ring Alejandro gave me. It'll be a minute before he realizes it's a fake."

My friend shook her head. "And when he discovers it, you'll be in a world of trouble."

"Not if he can't find me."

"Gloriana, running is never a good answer."

"Izzie, I have a child to protect. I'll do anything to accomplish it. We just need somewhere to go. Is there anyplace around New York?"

She sighed. "You know that I disagree with this. If you head north, I heard there's a small town there." My friend looked off into the distance. "I'll miss you."

"Same here." Coming back wasn't an option. Once people leave Havenwood Falls, the memories go away. They're unable to find their way back. Suddenly, I grabbed Izzie and hugged her tightly. "Think of it as an extended honeymoon. Oscar and I were having so much fun that we couldn't tear ourselves way."

Izzie sniffed. "I wish you didn't have to go."

"It's best." Not only was I protecting my unborn child and husband, I was protecting my friends. If no one knew where we were, they couldn't tell Alejandro or my family.

Since Oscar and I were planning to leave town for good, we spent the next few days hanging with those we cared about. It also gave me much-needed time to reproduce the Veleta keepsake. What I had to do required finesse and not some simple spell. I wanted it to hold up under inspection. At least, long enough for Oscar and me to make it across the country.

I held up the trinket to the light.

Hunter whistled low. "That's some hunk of jewelry. Is that really what it looked like?"

"Yeah. You know dragons. They love their bling." I placed the ring in a dust-covered black box and handed it to him. "That should convince him that you really had to look for it."

"I hope so. I'm riding down to Denver with Monte."

"Oh?"

Hunter tucked the box into his leather jacket. "How did Veleta find you in the first place?"

Good question. I shrugged. "I'd like to believe that someone tipped him off, but that makes no kind of sense. Most likely, he found my signature."

"Huh?" Hunter's brow furrowed.

"Brujas from my village are marked. It's supposed to enable a Cuélebra to find us," I admitted.

Hunter folded his arms over his chest. "And you forgot about that when you came here?"

"Yeah, I did. My parents told me about it, but I thought they were lying. No one else had ever left our village. I was in Denver for a year. When Alejandro didn't come for me, I thought I was safe."

"Fine." Hunter ran a hand through his hair. "You have to fix this, Gloriana. Remember, Veleta won't have any memories of this place. He won't even remember talking to you. Give me a note to go with the ring. I'll drop it off in Denver. Make it look like you came to your senses and called off the arrangement."

"Good thinking, but is Monte good going that far?" Not too long ago the shifter had a run-in with Death. The entity tied Monte and Pandora's souls together. What happens to one, happens to the other.

"He'll be fine. We'll only go for a day, and we're taking the truck."

"Good thinking."

Hunter surprised me and wrapped his arms around me. "I will miss you."

"Same here."

"You've been good for Izzie. Outside of Senora, her circle of friends was too small," the shifter admitted. "I know you won't be able to contact us but take care of yourselves."

I patted his back. "Do the same. You'll be at the celebration, right?"

"Naw. We'll head out in a few hours."

Reluctantly, I agreed and watched Hunter go out the front door. Then I remembered I had a party to get ready for.

All of our friends packed SIN's clubhouse. The latest rock music blared from the speakers while alcohol flowed freely. From a distance, I watched Liam and the fellas laughing and talking, and it made me sad. None of them would be a part of my child's life. A room full of good people, and we wouldn't be able to remember them.

A heavy hand landed on my shoulder. "Glori, if you want to change your mind, we can stay. We'll deal with Veleta."

I shook my head. "No. I don't want the stress of constantly looking for him. Addie said that she'll cover our trail. Alejandro won't be able to find us. Our child will grow up safe."

"You know this won't be the last time we have a gathering like this. Monte did some snooping around for me. Where we're headed, there's another MC. Two hellhounds run it."

Forcing a smile, I said, "Good. You won't feel like a total stranger."

"Glori, we won't lose Havenwood Falls. It will always be a part of us."

I knew that.

But there was something about that town tucked away in a box canyon that couldn't be duplicated. Maybe it was the magical waters found there. Maybe it was the people. Or maybe it was the history that many of the residents shared. Whatever it was, no matter where we lived next, it wouldn't compare to Havenwood Falls.

It was one minute to midnight, and Oscar decided to make a toast. The male of little words suddenly had much to say.

"As we say goodbye to this year and move into the next, remember those around you. Those who make your lives special. The new year is all about starting over. Starting fresh. From Gloriana and me, know that all of you will forever hold a place in our hearts."

"Here, here!" someone said.

The sounds of fireworks exploding could be heard.

"Happy New Year!" Liam announced.

Oscar came up to me with a glass of sparkling cider. "Happy New Year, Glori!"

"Happy New Year, baby!" I clinked my glass with his. "Here's to starting over."

"It's a new year and a new life for us."

We hope you enjoyed these short stories for the holidays. Stay up to date on all things Havenwood Falls at www.HavenwoodFalls.com

Subscribe to our reader group and receive free stories and more!

www.ingramcontent.com/pod-product-compliance
Lightning Source LLC
Chambersburg PA
CBHW030117260626
47156CB00008B/2696